WHAT DE

A collection of stories, i~~mages and~~ **third thing by Glenn Loury II**

Contents

204 Seconds 5
At the Foot of Olympus 7
On the Slope of Olympus 10
Peak Olympus 12
What Death Has Touched 16
The Priest 18
A Coming Storm 22
The Novel With No End 24
Desert Temptation 26
Mantra for a Dying World 28
Diaspora 30
Middle Passage 32
Birth of a Rebel 35
Mesa Shadows 37
Wise King Sulayman 38
The Splintered Child 41
Songs From the Damned 43
Book of Ellen 45
The New World 47
Under the Bed 49
Opere et Veritate 53
The Urn 54
End And Beginning 56
Creation Myths: The Dreamscape 58
The Scorpion and the Frog 60
It Gets Better 62
See No Evil, Hear No Evil 66
The Reflection 68
The Earthbound Shade 72
When the Wind Speaks... 75
Ashes to Ashes 78
The Historians 80

2nd Chance..82
The Perfect Fit...85

204 Seconds

In the corner stood brawny Arturo. Arturo, the prototype heavyweight—equally thick around the waist and chest, not a curve to his figure, just a straight line from shoulder to toe. He listens to a ticking clock only he can hear. Nose twitching—an arched and aching thing from a dozen old breaks—he wondered how he came to be a supporting player in his own life. A long arc lead him here, always the bass player, the silent scene partner, the prep cook. From the first moments—when he was born the quiet second twin to his bawling older brother Balto—to his marriage—where he and his equally timid wife were overshadowed by the bold proposal by the best man to the maid of (also Balto), he felt most comfortable in the shadows. And so it was still. Arturo, flinty enforcer, silently watched the Big Boss McGuin beat Art's own twin brother to death.

"Art…" The bludgeoned Balto whispered, his tone somewhere between plea and rebuke, "Art…"

Will you really just stand here? He asked himself. Doing nothing?

The meat-fisted McGuin, just as broad as the lunk Arturo if not nearly a head or two as high, himself had the same thought. Resting a moment from the once-over, he laughed, a wheezing, corrosive howl, and turned back to the silent Art.

"Maybe he'll listen to you, yeah? Don't twins have some kind uh… psychic connection er summat?" The cudgel in his hand was pointed right at Art, business end forward. McGuin flipped it effortlessly, displaying an agility that belied his bulk and presented the handle for Arturo to wield.

"Make 'im sing Art. Earn your Starbucks."

After the nastiest jobs, torture—or information extraction, as McGuin termed it—or murder—corp'real removal was the affable McGuin-ism—he always took the perpetrator of his mandated crimes out for coffee. Art stared at the cudgel, blinking slowly, remembering all the times he would have grabbed it gladly and bashed his brash brother Balto's skull in. His audacious proposal at the inauguration of Art's ill-fated marriage. All the times as kids when they wrestled and Balto always, always won.

"Those 204 seconds catch up to ya!" He'd laugh, referencing the difference in time between their births. "I can see your next move coming, before ya even think of it!" And he was right too. Two minutes and 24 seconds later, Art would close his eyes and see the fight unfold once more… from his Brother's perspective. Every move perfectly predicted, only after the fact instead of before. Alas, if only he had been the elder twin. Maybe then he might've become a star.

After each fight, Balto would tousle Art's hair affectionately and bound off on another adventure. A machine of perpetual motion, he sought the next thrill, the next surprise. Balto closed his eyes and saw the future. He closed his eyes and saw himself moving upwards towards brilliance. Up and up, until…

None of that energy remained in the battered man now. Not with both his legs, all ten fingers and ten toes, twisting in different directions. Not with his face a red mass and a dozen of his teeth on the floor. Art waited for the familial compassion to set in, waited for the instinct to refuse his task to rise. Yet his hand went to the proffered handle, and even then he expected to grasp it and bash McGuin's face in. He could just imagine rescuing his brother, killing the crime lord, all the while screaming "Who's the star now, eh? Who's the star?"

But he did none of those things. Slick wooden cudgel in hand, he walked over to his brother, trussed and moaning, and for a while said nothing at all. Then he bent down, to look his 'older' brother in the eye.

"Do me a favor brother, think for me on where the money is. I'll see it by and by."

"Art, pl-"

THWACK! Balto's head jolted back, eyes wide in shock for a moment, before they closed and his neck bent at a crooked angle. **SMOSH!** His skull grew a sudden dent, leaking fluids from a puncture made by jutting bone. Art let rise and fall the wooden weapon another half-dozen times, until the once identical siblings had very few features left in common. Balto's lungs filled with air a few more times; his heart let out a few more beats; his muscles twitched, perhaps out of instinct or his natural born stubbornness, before subsiding entirely.

In the room, only Art and a stunned McGuin remained.

"Christ," Stammered McGuin, "Did ya really? Did ya have to-Christ, Art! I mean, it was only a little bit o'money, but… well, Christ!"

Art didn't respond, he dropped the cudgel at the feet of the lifeless mass once named Balto, a man he once loved, before retreating back to his corner. Back to the shadows. For a few moments, he didn't say anything, then he checked his watch.

"Give me… two and a half minutes boss. I'll tell you where your money is."

At the Foot of Olympus

They gathered at the mountain's base, seven pilgrims. All there for different reasons. A father and son, mirror images of each other. Their faces cast in the hard-set of grief. The son's hair was frizzy and brown, the father's thinner and greyed. Both wore the long unkempt beards of many months of travel. An elderly woman, at first glance she appeared a frail thing just clinging to life, but the others knew better. Only the strong could make this journey. Only the determined got this far. Two children, brother and sister, checked their packs for the climb ahead. They were idiosyncrasies equal to the elderly woman, two adolescents, but again, the look in their eyes presaged a loss that would age any soul.

The last two travelers—a young woman with high cheekbones, freckles on her sunburnt nose and hollow eyes who stared mutely into the middle distance and an infant swaddled to her chest who slumbered and gurgled and never once cried—stood apart from the others. She wore the child like a backpack, seemingly unaware that it lived. For the child's part, he seemed to want for nothing.

They assembled at the foot of Olympus and waited for the sign their journey was to begin. Father and Son did little to hide their unease at the other's presence.

"Are you sure you're able to-" Son started to ask the Old Woman, but her glare stopped him dead. Her look said more clearly than words: *Mind your own business, boy, as I do mine.*

"Well, we all have our reasons, I suppose." He muttered to himself, shaking his head ruefully.

Father tried to help the children tending to their rations and clothing, but Brother snapped at him, barking like a mad dog. Sister did not even raise her eyes to meet his gaze or answer his offers of aid. The middle-aged widower backed away with his hands up, showing he meant no harm. Exchanging a look with his son, a whole conversation passed between them in silence. Their fellow travelers were best left alone. This was no picaresque tale. They would trade no stories about the losses and hardships that brought them here. Their journey would not be peppered with the episodic remembrances of truth-seekers.

Yes, he imagined very well that he already knew their stories. If not the specifics, at the very least their flavor. And he knew that he would be no more inclined to share the details of his pain than they were.

Even now, years later, Father saw, clear as day, Mother's hand squeezing his one last time and going slack. He remembered how frail she was. How she looked just as anguished in death, frozen in the last moment of pain. He remembered the hospice caregiver's last words: "She's with God now, son." Small comfort. Did God love her any more than they had? He very much doubted it. He looked up to the mountain's peak, shrouded always in clouds, and wondered if the countless others who made the legendary ascent had found their answers up in the cold.

Either way, soon his suffering would end.

He patted Son gently on the shoulder, lead him away to erect their tent and wait for dark.

The group split into four sections, waiting in a clearing between the forest at Olympus' base and a quiet lake. Its waters shimmered blue and orange, reflecting the sky. Wind whispered ripples across its surface. It howled in the travelers' ears, and each of them were reminded of a different loss. Or the same loss from different perspectives. Father and Son sat around a makeshift fire pit, heating a simple dinner of ground meal and dried salted meat. They ate and talked of simple things, of their memories of Mom and Wife. Of their aches and pains. Of preparations for the morrow.

The Elder sat, her back against a spindly oak, working with her thin fingers at spinning something out of yarn. It was a long, multi-hued woolen beast. Once it may have been intended as a scarf, but that had been years ago. Now it was merely her finger's obsession, something to pass the time. A project she would add to until she died.

Brother and Sister, their losses temporarily forgotten, played on the pier that cut partway into the lake. Each trying to push the other in. Laughing, they fell in together and swam beneath the clear, calm water.

Mother and Child also stood on the pier, Mother still staring blankly, child still sleeping and murmuring in its dreams. No one came near her. Somehow they sensed hers may well be the saddest story of them all. What answers did she demand from God? Why bring the child?

After a fashion, night began to fall. The sun set behind the mountain and the group was left in darkness, segmented. The Siblings scratched stick figure patterns into the dirt with rocks. Father and Son prepared to sleep, in case they were not called for before morning. The Elder knitted, never stopping, as if the action itself were all she needed for sustenance. Mother and Child had not moved in hours.

Thunder clapped from the mountain peak, preceded by flashes like lightning. This sound and fury fell not from the skies but the mountain itself. A giant Tesla Coil. The travelers assembled, three pairs and the Elder, eager for whatever came next. One bolt struck the ground right before them, cracking loud and smelling of burning ions. It tore the ground asunder, shrieking and groaning as the Earth trembled. They covered their eyes and shrank from the noise and brightness.

When the dust settled, and the smoke cleared, a voice greeted them.

"Seven have come. Seven seeking answers to questions beyond our purview. They seek the wisdom of a God they no longer revere. Welcome to Olympus."

A stooped man, even older than the Elder seeker, stood in the cracked Earth's hollow. Whether he had traveled by lightning strike, or been hidden in the Earth beneath their feet they did not know. He continued, the smile on his face at odds with his solemn words and task. As if, at his advanced age, there was nothing new to see. As if the only amusement he took in this world came from the expected.

"This is the Rubicon. Beyond this point there is no return. Only forward, only answers to questions you may end up wishing you did not know. Ignorance is… bliss, they say."

He turned and walked through the trees towards the mountain. The old man began to ascend. Slowing when he sensed that none followed, still dazed by his entrance, still rubbing the dots from their eyes and the ringing from their ears, he called over his shoulder.

"The time to come is now. If I pass out of eyeshot, you will never see me again. You will die, lost on this mountain."

For the first time, each pilgrim met the other's eye. Everyone nodded their affirmation. The unspoken camaraderie… we traveled too far to turn back now.
One by one, they began to climb. Towards truth. Towards sweet death.

On the Slope of Olympus

Every mountain evokes a tragic tale. Beginning, as all tragedies do, with a broad foundation, a base of emotion. You rise, towards a narrowing peak. Everything leads to the highest point, the loss you cannot see until it is upon you. Once you climb the mountain, and your heart has rent in twain, you can look down. Past the thinning tree line, the scraggly oaks, the brooks that feed the streams that feed the rivers, the water always rushing down, down. You look past the mountain and see the whole of the land, and you see how inevitable it was that you came to be here. You see the leavings of all that fell away from you, the slow dying of the bereaved. And you look up to find that nothing remains. Nothing but the hollow feeling that has become all you are.

This Father thought, numb to the cold, deaf to the nattering guide that lead them towards God.

The brief moment of camaraderie had long been forgotten by the seven pilgrims, the seven mourning souls driven here by their need for answers. Indeed, as they climbed together, shuffling through dirt, tripping over weed and underbrush, they had never felt more separate from one another and from the world they left behind. Silently, they judged, each not recognizing their arrogance reflected in the others.

How dare they? How dare they encroach on *my* search for peace?

The old man, their surprisingly surefooted guide, prattled on, though his words contradicted his cheery tone. "Five minutes, not a second more, not a second less. Every question you can have answered in that span you can ask. At the end of your time, together we will decide if you can be allowed to leave. Or if you will join the legion of the waiting. We will decide if you are worthy."

Strange sentiments, and since they meant nothing to the assembled—outside of the fact that they will be allowed to ask the question burning in each heart—they ignored them as they scrabbled up Olympus' backside. Brother and Sister held hands. If one fell, the other helped him or her up. They did not cry. Neither were left with tears to spare. Brother stopped briefly to watch a rat snake slithering past in the grass.

Mama, he mouthed. Mama?

She showed them how to trap small game once, in a wood sandwiched between two Appalachian Mountains. How best to bait them. How to find the common trails used by rabbits, squirrels, hares and woodchucks. How to move silently through these woods. It had been some years in the orphanage since, but slowly memories returned to them.

He watched the snake who regarded him in kind, unblinking and not moving its flat-black head. Brother made to creep low and quiet towards its home in the knoll, to wring the life from it f\as Mama taught him, but was pulled away gently by Sister. She shook her head sadly, not wasting words on what her reproving gaze made clear. No, they whispered, remember why we are here.

We will ask God why together.

Never looking up from her ever growing mess of yarn, the Elder didn't miss a step up the mountain side that sloped steadily upward. Though her task consumed her, her feet had eyes of their own.

Quiet steps for the quiet Mother and her unnaturally happy child. Father could not figure this infant, seemingly warm in the cold, never hungry, never needing to be held. The longer they walked, the longer its Mother continued to ignore the life on her back, a suspicion grew: this 'child', this thing, whatever it was, was not human. He caught the boy watching him back, surreptitious glances from beneath the swaddling clothes. The babe wore the conniving smile of a far older man, grey eyes gleaming with sharp intelligence.

They ascended in silence. The air thinned, their flesh chilled and their souls soured. Passing the tree line, they forest shrink and shrivel in the distance. Flora that survived the oxygen poor atmosphere managed small lives, clinging to the rocky slope like gangrenous limbs mid-amputation—only attached by sinew and ligament—like a stiff wind would send them tumbling back down the mountainside.

Yet they remained. As did the pilgrims, climbing past brambles towards the apex of their grief, God and the summit.

Peak Olympus

Gradually they came to the peak and only then did their journey begin. The nattering old man, in a tan robe that brushed the ground, stopped and turned to his flock as they cleared the last outcropping of rocks. From here the pilgrims looked down and saw nothing but clouds. The enormity of the task before them consumed all else. Nothing remained but the question. Nothing but what they set out to accomplish: confronting God. Demanding answers for the enormity of loss.

"Why. We must understand why." Man, woman and child each had the same thought in the silence.

The skies were clear, yet snow covered the flattened peak. The elder smiled, forgetting her tangled mass of yarn for a moment to run her hand through the sleet. It was fine and cold, melting quickly in her hands. Olympus's top was a smooth dome and reminded her of her balding husband, whose hair had melted white, and then away to nothing as the decades passed. Still he refused to embrace age, clinging to what frizz remained as he approached his eight decade. He died in the bathroom, applying balm to his scalp purported to encourage hair growth. She buried him in a full, brown wig. It was what he would have wanted.

Why? Why wasn't I first? She closed her eyes, dropped her white knitting onto the white Earth, and awaited an answer.

To the others who walked with her, trudging up the slope as she had, seeking answers as she did, it appeared that she stepped forward, dropped her yarn, and disappeared into the open air. They did not gasp, numbed as they were by their own losses, but merely waited. Waited for her to resurface, or for their own audience to begin. For her part, the elder did not know she was transported. Only that the sun rose, that a beam shining bright obliterated the world around her.

If you were first. You would not be here. I require your strength, forged in grief. Step forward my daughter and be healed.

The Elder watched her hands, watched the decades and the wrinkles melt away. Then her skin itself grew translucent. She felt light, became light, opened her eyes and saw a legion of billions standing before her. She smiled. Home, she was home. There, at the end of the first row, smiled a familiar, balding face.

The Mother placed her silent babe on the snow. He protested this cool embrace no more than he did anything else, accepting the world with wise gray eyes. Instead he watched as she walked, palms up in supplication, towards Olympus's center.

"You cursed me!" She said aloud, eyes brimming with tears, voice quavering with madness. "You took away my husband, he who loved me best. Birthed me this... creature! Strapped to my back like a lodestone. I suffer and I must know why! Why this unnatural birth? Why take from me my one true l-"

Midsentence, she too disappeared, and the others shifted uneasily from foot to foot, waiting for her to return.

He looks at me and knows my thoughts. I hear in my head a child's voice calling me the loving names of my husband, taken from me in the throes of pregnancy. Why?

The heady power of lost lovers, it builds between you even as you, unknowingly, cradle him in your arms. Look into your child's eyes Mother, and tell me what you see.

From the obscuring mist, she turned and looked at him, serene even in frost.
No, it cannot be. He cannot be...

Chance thwarts even my intentions at times. Your love's accident was not in my plans, yet there is always another path. You two were meant to be together. To be together and serve me. Pick him up. Pick up your child—and come hither.

The Mother bent from the mist towards the babe she once feared. He frowned up at her, as if to say "Now, do you know me?"

"Of course I do," She whispered. "Husband... son. Partner in life and thereafter."

To the others on the mount, it seemed as if her torso emerged briefly, reclaiming the life she once thought lost forever. There, in the fog, they took their place in the growing legion.

Father and Son grew uneasy. It was one thing to commit oneself to confronting God's might; it was wholly another to witness it firsthand. There was a force here that consumed them one by one. Its eye focused on them next. They felt it sweep them into the past, back into the hospital room. Back to the day that sent them hurtling down this course, through the cold and into the light. They too disappeared. Brother, Sister and Guide stood on Olympus Peak alone, the siblings waiting their turn, the guide hidden behind a knowing smile.

Father and Son, in a white room beside her once more. The clean smell of death settled around them, an old forgotten friend they now faced again. Time passed, nurses and doctors filtering in and out, easing her pain, speaking words that passed around them unabsorbed. Words they heard and responded to, but at the same time did not fully comprehend. They crept closer and closer towards the inevitable. Knowing, yet not knowing, seeing, yet refusing to see. The days, they passed so slowly. The end, it came all at once.

She had not spoken all day. The night before, after crying for hours, a nurse administered morphine for her pain. Now she only breathed, short, racking breaths, forced from her in spurts. In each gasp there was a little less life. Father stood by the window, unable to look at the beating corpse that was once his beloved. Son sat by the bed, holding her hand, reading her favorite cheesy mystery. The seconds crept by, each an eternity, each the briefest instant they would never get back. They relived this scene, they endured, both within and without themselves, wondering what they might change. Cursing themselves for not appreciating each moment, committing it to memory.

These were the final minutes. Torture, paradise, all they had.

The passing itself was not dramatic thing. One minute she was there, the dying Mother, the decrepit wife. The next she sighed, a brief hiccup, and was gone. Two, three seconds passed in disbelief. Had she squeezed his hand before she went? Did her eyes flutter briefly and focus on her husband's face? Had they imagined it? Son blinked, thinking he might find himself back at home, and discover that the last few months were nothing but a dream. But alas, he opened his eyes and there he was and there she was not. Only a cooling mass remained where once there was everything.

Grief rushed into the void, loud and violent and hungry grief. Father and Son held each other and wailed, but to no avail. No amount of performative mourning would replace what they had lost. A pit opened up in both of them. A pit they papered over with this quest. Here, bowed before God, the wound was exposed once more and bled afresh.

They sobbed, and the voice spoke. Three words were all it took.

She is waiting.

They saw her, hale and beaming. They nodded and were subsumed.

On the peak of Olympus, the mountain of God, Brother and Sister stood and waited. The wind cracked around their heads. Clouds gathered and in the wild air, it once again began to snow. A voice spoke from the gray.

Step forward.

Holding hands, glances resolute, they walked toward the mountaintop's center. They saw a familiar smile, heard a laugh they thought lost forever. They too disappeared.

Now alone, after waiting a moment to see if any would reappear, the guide departed, hiking back down through the frigid drifts with a knowing smile.

What Death Has Touched

"'Tis a fearful thing, to love what death can touch."

For as long as life can be, for as many long and painful silences that we endure, however many days and nights pass and seem unending. The lives of men and women ultimately boil down to a few key moments, none more important or more futile than the last. It was in such a moment Farouk found himself when he woke, bound to a chair, in a room full of smoke, a lilting voice reciting his favorite poem as if it were song.

The world froze, and he looked around the room in a daze. Flames hung in the air, frozen in their rapid consumption of the wallpaper, of his bookshelves and furniture and carpet, of his world entire. The air hung hot and heavy, searing his lungs with each breath. In the shadows, another figure moved, he squinted to make it out. Though as the man spoke, his blood ran cold. The familiar words of Halevi bringing little comfort.

"A fearful thing, to love, to hope, to dream, to be –"

"Ti?" Farouk called into the dark, the pet name of his ex-lover Tichaun, knowing it was him but not wanting it to be all the same. "Ti? What are yo-"

He danced lithely out from the shadows, nearly indistinguishable from them. The sweat on his obsidian skin glistened with the firelight. Caressing Farouk's cheek with his hand, he spun around the chair, then spun the chair around, so his old flame could see that flames surrounded them. Once this moment ended, so too would their lives.

"to be... and oh, to lose." The man smiled as he straddled Farouk, he wore no clothes and, despite his situation, the bound man felt a growing warmth inside at his lover's familiar closeness. The man was nude... and as beautiful as he was deranged. Their position together inspired memories of happier times.

"Ti. You-you don't have to do this. We can still, we can still..." Lies faded from Farouk's tongue as futility hit him like a bullet train. What was done had already been done; there is no going back, only forward into the end. He closed his eyes, remembering the look on Tichaun's face when he walked in on Farouk with one of the Egyptian scholar's students. He said nothing, not interrupting the liaison, only slipping back outside once he was sure Farouk had seen him there, that there was a witness to this crime against love.

Until now, Farouk had not seen him again, assuming he had found some other diversion. Like the wind he was always flying, laughing, speaking like behind his words there was a melody only he could hear. But now... now...

"A thing for fools this. And a holy thing." As Tichaun spoke, Farouk felt the room grow hotter. Behind his lover, a shadow against the crimson burning, he saw the flames again begin to move. Sweat mottled the hair that covered the back of his hands, black bristles on hands brown like earthen clay.

"Ti... I'm sorry. I said I would be better and I wasn't. I'm sorry. This moment is more than I deserve."

Ti smiled, and with one hand tilted Farouk's head until their lips met in a kiss. As their mouths explored each other one last time, as the flames grew closer, as it grew harder and harder to breathe in the smoke. The Egyptian heard his lover's voice, as if his larynx commanded the air itself.

"For your life has lived in me, your laugh once lifted me, your word was gift to me."

Flames licked their skin, consuming them in desperate search of fuel, melting flesh and bone into blackened carbon, fusing them into the one they never were in life. Farouk felt no pain; only distant regret; he only thought:

To remember this brings painful joy.

And then the moment ended, and so came another, and another. And another.

After hours of moments, as police sifted through the ash trying to differentiate between what was once man and once house, wind sung its way through the home's skeletal remains, sifting the ash with playful hands. Had any officers turned to see the ash winding its way across the charred floor, they would have seen—for a brief moment—this final moment's words flash in the dying embers before dissipating.

Tis a human thing, love,
a holy thing, to love
what death has touched.

The Priest

God works in mysterious ways. Man, the monster in his image. What a dark creature he calls to work his will.

The bathwater, warm and red, lapped pleasantly against their bodies in the dimming light. Was that the candle dying, or his eyesight fading? The Priest could no longer tell as his eyelids fluttered slowly. So slowly. It was as if the world slowed, as if time ground to a halt, but he knew it was mere perception as life trickled from his veins and into the overflowing bath. The rosewater trickled and splashed onto the tile floor, the water made rose by the lives of the two men within. Yes, the Priest thought again, God works in mysterious ways.

He recalled the first time he was commanded by the Lord to serve.

The Priest was a child, no more than 5, a yowling rebel, a terror to his poor parents and siblings who watched over him with the fraying patience of the most tested saints. He was a terror… until one night he dreamt of desert. One he had never seen in life, of endless sand, of dunes that twisted in the wind, where piano music played in the distance, carried to his ears diegetically by the breeze. Satie's 1st Gymnopedie, a favorite of his mother to play while she stroked her swollen belly where the Father-to-be waited for his moment to be born.

Come to me.

And so boy walked towards the call, in his dreams a hobbled old man with aged face and weathered hands, until he saw b a figure. A formless shadow whose dark hands danced effortlessly across a piano perched delicately on the dunes. Its eyes were two lights that hanging in the void where a face should be, which held no other features that the Priest could see. The piece finished, though the notes lingered in the air long after its hands left the keys. The figure turned to face the Boy-cum-Old Man, who somehow knew he was in the presence of his Creator.

"Oh my God…" He whispered in a voice creakier than he remembered. Knees shaking, he fell prostrate on the sand, suddenly feeling all 70-80 of the extra years the dream had placed on him. "Oh my God. Oh my God. God. God."

Honor thy father and mother.

Like the music, the voice seemed to come from the air. A dark and heavy thing, yet not unkind. Not demanding, but with the plainness of one who knew their commands would be obeyed.

"God, I-"

Honor thy father and mother.

And suddenly the Priest saw himself, as the Creator saw him, as his parents and loved ones must have seen him. As ungrateful and angry, a whirlwind of destruction. He wept. Only five and already his life was so steeped in sin.

"Yes Lord," He sobbed. "I shall. I shall obey. I will be your light in the world."

And he woke in his bed, seeing his room, the world and himself as if for the first time. And from that time on his was the model son and sibling.

One night, ten years later, after a night of shameful fumbling with his own most private of parts, fantasizing about formless darkness, the teenager met the Lord again in his slumber. Again he was an old man, falling at once prostrate on the hot sand. Again the soft piano tremored music through the air. There was no doubt in his mind he would serve, whatever his God asked.

You must serve me and no others. The darkness commanded.

"Yes Lord," The old man acquiesced in a phlegmy tone, as his unnaturally aged joints throbbed rheumatically. "If I may, God…" He began, not lifting his eyes.

Silence was his only answer.

Licking his lips to moisten them in the dry-heat of his dreamscape, the Priest to become continued. "If I may… how do you want me t-"

You must serve me, and no others. As the Lord responded, the Priest saw in his mind's eye the man he was expected to become. A serious man. A somber man in the trappings of piety, who had forgone the needs of the flesh to serve the aesthetic vision of God. He was to take the sacred oath.

"I see my Lord, I see your will. And I will become it."

And so he studied the good book, consumed Augustine, Tertullian and the exegeses of Origen. He forgot desire, or suppressed the remembering of his youthful and became a man of the cloth. One known as the most pious and most high.

And for a time, he was content. And the Lord was silent.

Then, 25 years later, a young man walked into his confessional. One he had seen in his church, lurking at the beginning of a service the week before, but had left. Something about the young man, his shock of curly black air, his soft brown eyes, his full lips, his troubled innocence, captured the Priest. He was striking, beautiful even. The color of his oak pews, and skin just as smooth as those varnished seats. He could tell by his darting expression that this young man, still mostly a boy, was in a dark place. Maybe it was a place from where he and the Lord still could pull him out. He thought of counseling the man, and something in him stirred. Something long forgotten. Desire.

Standing before a crowded congregation in that moment, the Priest was desperately glad he wore a flowing robe.

The priest tried to put the 'man' out of his mind then. Some dark force was testing him. Until that fateful night. When that beautiful boy walked back into his church and entered the confessional to lay bare his sins.

"Forgive me father for I have sinned. It has been… well, I've never confessed."

The Priest coughed to clear his throat. "I'm listening my son. Tell me your sins."

Tell me your sins. Why did the prospect of sin suddenly excite him so? The Priest shifted uncomfortably on the bench, needing to adjust himself. Afraid that the boy would see. Thrilled by the chance that he might.

The man, eager to unburden himself, started right from the beginning. "Well, as a child, I was terrible to my parents. I lied often. I stole. I-"

The Priest, he tried to listen, but was too captivated by the hint of the boy he could see through the wooden slats. His well-formed body. His mouth that listed a litany of horrors, yet beckoned him toward unknown pleasures. He closed his eyes, and felt himself back in the heat. In the dying wind. The quiet notes of Satie called to him on the breeze. Unlike in his previous dreams, it was night, and the soothing music took on an ominous lilt in the darkness.

Against the starless sky, it was almost impossible to see the Lord, a shadow in absolute black. The music this time, it felt like a parting, a mournful goodbye to the dreams that had come before.

The aged priest, still so far from the man in his dreams, yet much older than the boy who first became God's servant, took to his knees. "What would you have me do? Are you… testing me my Lord? How can I serve you? How do you want me to serve you?"

The shadow did not stop playing, yet the music grew more distant. The sand between them seemed to stretch and grow, an expanse of death—the gulf, so vast, that has always separated God from humankind. The Priest never felt it more acutely than he did in that moment.

"I want to serve you, oh God. But I also want-"

Sin. The desert grew so wide between the two that the Priest could no longer see the dark God he served. *So much sin. You humans steep yourself in it, bathe in the filth like fleas. You want to serve, boy?*

The world grew so dark, the Priest could not see his own hands pass in front of his face. The music faded, the only notes those of his breath—ragged and shallow. "Yes, God, you know it."

Then purge yourself. And suddenly the Priest saw a window into the asked-for future, he and the boy embracing. First in the church, then unclothed in bed, then in the bath… their eyes vacant and unseeing. Crimson water spilling out from the bath all around them, pooling around them on the floor. Flooding the room with their spent lives.

Purge yourself of sin, and come to me.

The Priest opened his eyes, and shook his head, back in the world, back swimming in his latent desires.

"Father? Did you hear what I just said?"

"Sorry my child, please say that again."

The Priest could see through the slats as the young man licked his full lips in fear, trepidation… anticipation. The man of God knew what was coming, he feared it. But knew he dare not defy the Lord All Mighty, the darkness who directed his light.

"I was speaking, Father, of my most recent sin."

"Go on, my son."

"One of desire… forbidden desire."

"And who did you desire, my son?" The Priest asked, hearing the answer before it was spoken. *A Man of God.*

"A Man of God, Father." The young man, the boy, was now quite boldly meeting the Priest's gaze through the lattice slats of the confessional. And somehow the Priest knew without looking in a mirror that the hunger he saw there was reflected by the need in his own. He rose, left the confessional, walking back through the oak pews to the door to his quarters hidden behind the altar. He ignored the judgmental gazes of the Father, the Son and the Holy Ghost, the silent admonition of the Mother and the Whore. He did not need to look back to know the boy followed; he could hear his steps echo on the stone.

They entered the small room, empty but for a desk and small mattress that lay on the floor covered in fraying, threadbare sheets. The boy closed the door behind them and for a while they did not speak, staring at each other, consuming each other. Silent but for heavy breaths.

Then they came together, and, after a fashion, came—together.

They lay together on the bed, and The Priest savored this moment. The glow he felt unmatched by anything except that first moment in the Desert with his Dark God: who spun Satie gently into the air; who spoke him into a humble life of devoted service. One of servile delight now hurtling to a dark end. He rose, still naked and still tumescent, and led the boy by the hand, docile after their coupling. Perhaps in awe of a man of God who could ravish him thus. Perhaps at some level aware that he was but an offering.

He led him down a corridor and into the bathroom. He filled the tub with hot steaming water; got in, and beckoned the young man to sit in the scalding water. And as he did so took him into his arms. The boy's eyes were closed, lips spread into a grin of guileless bliss. As if he too had been unburdened of his sins. His eyes were still closed when the Father picked up the straight razor he always left by the tub so he could shave as he watched. His body barely jolted as the Priest drew a wider, redder smile into the soft brown flesh of his neck. The boy shook only a few times before lying still in his Father's arms, his life quickly spent in the dirtied bath water.

"I'm sorry my boy," He whispered, before running the razor up the veins in both of his own arms, spilling his redness into the water, which quickly ran the color of the darkest rose. The waters-displaced by their slackened bodies—tumbled over the tub's edge, staining the church bathroom's tile with his final sin.

As he lay there, as time flattened and wound to a halt, as his days of service came to their close, again he heard the music. It drowned out all other sound, that quiet piano, that holy musing of Satie, that call of his dark Lord

What a dark creature he calls to work his will. Man, the monster in his image.

Yes. The Priest thought. *God works in mysterious ways.*

Then at last, he closed his eyes.

A Coming Storm

"No one could ever say where The Rains first came from; we only knew that they would never cease."

As the barge cut through the fog, rain beat on its steel hull with the muted staccato of distant timpanis—a calming lullaby to the increasingly drunk Captain Lawash. Clotted rust's stench, mixed with stale salt-water, choked her senses. No matter how many years she spent at sea, she never became noseblind to its rot. She never adjusted to the slow accumulation of scents, gathering like the water that leaked through the rivets which held her vessel together.

The captain finished her flask and lay back on her bunk, her mattress hard like a stone. Rainwaters sloshed around the inside of her skull, throwing her off-balance with their constant patter against her brain. All she wanted was for the world to stop spinning, but the more she drank, the faster it turned.

She swam through hooch and memories of her youth. Closing her eyes, she saw the world as it was then, bathed in a pleasant yellow glow. Dew-streaked grass tickled her bare feet as she danced through her parents' backyard. Marcy, the family dog, sniffed at her face, large wet snout touching her diminutive and dry nose. They watched her, Mom and Dad, from the doorway, smiling. Her mother's arm wrapped loose around her father's waist, in the easy manner they had with one another.

When she was nine, the sun disappeared under roiling clouds, beneath endless layers of drab blues and gray. The Rains began to fall, fittingly enough, as she waded in the ocean at the beach. Watching the distant ocean waves that would one day be her home—that would soon consume the Earth entire—she let her Dad lead her away. "Don't worry, Silly," He calmed her as she pouted, "We'll come back another day."

They never did. In the coming weeks, as the nature of the crisis became clear. He was called away to study the coming emergency. Frightened nations convened a global institute of pre-eminent climatologists who found nothing but questions with no answers. Where did the precipitation originate? How could the storm spread across the whole globe? When would it end?

How would humanity adapt if it never did?

"How fah we've fallin'..." She slurred and smacked her lips, "How fah are we still t'fall?"

Inebriation swaddled her better than her threadbare sheets ever could. Her mouth and head contained more cotton than the rags she shivered through. Her body screamed for water, but—even though as captain, she could easily requisition another liter—she dare not claim more than her fair share.

Indeed, how far they had fallen. Cursed to drift through watery damnation, measuring every drink they took.

Her crew had precious few hours to work before they themselves had to retreat to their cabins, these men and women, and secure themselves against the danger to come. A storm approached, well, a storm fiercer than that which was always among them. Her meteorologist came to her early that afternoon with presentiments of calamity.

"I see it in the clouds Ma'am. The ones we enter are mighty angry. Up to 125 kn." He showed her calculations she could never quite wrap her head around, and then satellite images that were far clearer. Hurricane storm clouds barred their way to the Conclave

She nodded shakily, buzzed even then. Her nips of that hip flask started earlier and earlier each day. Gordon, always by her side when not overseeing the dispensation of her orders, knew without being asked what was to be done.

"I'll see to it we start taking the appropriate measures captain."

On Gordon's sturdy shoulder, she lay a trembling hand.

"Thank you, Gord. I'm counting on you."

He saluted, but could not hide the hurt in his eyes. The gulf between them grew wider every day. It grew, along with the gap between who she was now and the effective seaman she used to be. More and more she was consumed by her pain, fleeing from the burden of command into a bottle.

Responsibility, it wore her down to a nub.

Waiting for sleep, she imagined that over the deluge, she could hear her crew. A few dozen men and women worked through the night above, bearing their most precious cargos below deck and lashing everything else to the transport ship's flatbed. Gordon, the boatswain, would be working them hard, drenching them in sweat as well as the ever present rain. Beneath her, in the stokehold, men and women drenched in sweat and with painted faces eased off the steam engines, slowing the barge's pace to a crawl. Beneath them, horticulturists tended to their sustainable garden, the manufactured environment where they grew all their crops. Alongside them were biologists and veterinarians who prepared their livestock for the coming turbulence with gentle whispers, medicine and heavy doses of tranquilizers.

Around her, the men and women whose lives depended on her stewardship worked, as she receded further into the fogs of drunkenness and sleep, wondering at the weakness of person she had become.

"I wa'nt always like this," She spoke to the remorseful ghosts. Every soul dead under her care watched her every night, silent and reproachful. Each loss had taken another piece of her, until most of her strength lay strewn about the ocean bottom and only a shell remained.

This small part of her, this part that still lived, as she slipped into the comatose slumber of self-medication, hoped for the worst with surprising clarity.

Perhaps this storm will claim us. Perhaps this pain can end...
...Mom, Dad, I'll see you again someday. Hopefully someday soon.

The Novel With No End

It whispered...
The sun set and another deadline flew by. Impatient editors demanded he produce the manuscript. Their e-mails and texts buzzed in his ear. Yet, no matter what he wrote, despite the fact that every scene and action found its way into his novel, he was no closer to an end. The next great American project, his multi-genre magnum opus wandered lost, totally separated from cohesiveness. The book was about everything, about nothing, a monster now approaching 300,000 words. No matter how hard he tried, no matter how rigorously he outlined and storyboarded the action, he drew no closer to a conclusion.

Through the fog, a shape wavered. A dark and ominous presence in the mist. Somehow he knew it, but could not find its name. The creature reached for him in the dark, with prehensile limbs and uncertain intent. It whispered... it whispered...

The author stopped typing, stymied. What did it whisper, and why? What even was the 'it'? Where was this going? This coda seemed so unnecessary so unrelated to the rest of the plot, and yet some force compelled him to affix this passage at the end of an otherwise complete text. It demanded he obsess over this seemingly needless paragraph, a vestigial appendage dangling from his manuscript.

Complete with introduction, rising action and climax, the plot of his book had resolved. Characters' nuances and motives made plain by 400 pages of perspicacious text. Lovers were joined and lost. They died and in death found themselves in the other's arms again. Wandering the indefinite fog of plot, battling antagonist and protagonist alike, they endured. They changed; they grew. And the more they grew, the more their essence remained the same. And then the tale ended. The tale ended... until into it wandered fog, his lost protagonist far from home and the creature whispering faintly in the night. There at the precipice he sat, trapped by infinite possibility.

Desperate, the author pored over every page, searching his own words for clues to the finish. Where had he gone wrong?

Through the fog...
Years passed. Publishing houses abandoned him to his self-imposed exile. A brilliant mind succumbed to the madding dark, they muttered. What a shame, such a loss. Still he stared, oblivious to the civilization that left him behind, at the same forty two words, a paragraph with no end. A thesis with no conclusion. Marks on the page, time robbed them of their meaning. Now they were little more than mere totems of his failure.

He closed his eyes, and, as he did daily, tried once again to visualize this creature in the dark. This beast, it whispered a message of the utmost importance, both for his protagonists and for himself. If only he could hear, if only he could see. But alas he heard only murmurs, saw the barest hint of form. The indefinite creature loomed over an unsure end. The author wept.

Then, out of the blue, as inspiration is wont to do, an idea struck. One only born in a man divorced from his senses.

"This... doesn't have to end," He spoke, wheezing in a voice rusted by disuse.

So inspired, he slapped his laptop back to life and typed:

Through the fog, a shape wavered. A dark and ominous presence in the mist. Somehow he knew it, but could not recall its name. The creature reached for him in the dark, with prehensile limbs and uncertain intent. It whispered... it whispered...

"I cannot hear you," *The hero spoke.* "Come closer..."

The creature did not move, nor did it raise its voice. He entreated it again.

"Please, I must know what you say."

Stock still it stood; features still obscure. Its outline was just barely visible in the night's gloom and the fog.

"Please."

Please...

Desert Temptation

On the forty-first night, the tempter once again visited the desert. He wore the form of a buzzard, circling around the wasted figure that dragged itself through the dunes.

"These constant tests. What kind of creature is so unsure of its subjects that he must test their fidelity again and again?"

The bird hopped closer and closer as it spoke.

"We could be kings, you and I. The world would open to us like a lotus in bloom. All you need do is kneel down and worship me instead of him."

The buzzard grew to many times its size, and clutched the frail son of God in its talons. He did not fight, though he wished to with all his heart. He was too weak. Hunger plagued his every thought, hunger and thirst and… doubt. Ascending through the clouds, the creature of darkness continued its pitch.

"What has he done for you that I cannot do? Birthed you and abandoned you in this land of men? You know what he has in store. Dreams of laceration and crucifixion, I've seen them. Your God, he will feed you to these creatures. And for what—their salvation?"

Approaching the snowy peak of a high mountain, the buzzard set him down gently in the frigid wasteland.

"He is gone, if ever he was there. Left you to your fate: Death among those who will pay you lip-service for centuries. Who will use your name as an excuse for their own hatreds. Tell me, where is the divine in that?"

The buzzard began to shrink and transform. Talons turned into feet, dark and calloused. Wings became hands, hard yet perfectly manicured. His beady eyes became fuller, but did not lose their smolder. He did not grow clothes, but stood in the shadows, naked and roped with muscle. He approached the fallen Son of God, who shivered. Walking through the snow, the Prince of Darkness gave no sign he himself noticed the cold.

"Your father, up on high, offers you nothing but pain. I offer-" The black prince paused to smile, "-something more."

He helped the Son to his feet. They stood at the mountain's peak, looking down at the world. As if sensing their gaze, the clouds fled, allowing them a glimpse of Earth and all its kingdoms. The Prince's hands caressed him, and the Son felt a warmth unlike any he had felt before. He tried to remember his Mother's face. Her words, telling him of his great and terrible fate. Their comfort felt so far away.

"He demands our forgiveness, promises us a grand paradise. I have been there, O Loyal Son. It is as quickly taken away as it is granted. We are as easily cast from His grace as taken to His bosom." The Prince choked on every 'He' and 'His' like they were the greatest curse he could use. In his dark eyes burned a mad fire, a dark hatred for the Creator. This anguish, it repelled and attracted the son. The doubts, they mirrored his own. Those he dared never admit, even to himself on bleak nights.

Looking at his own hands, the frail son began to contemplate the power he wielded, and the things he might do. Wonders he could achieve and, for once, in his own name. For his own sake and his own gain. What is life, if the only point is to die for others? He began to listen to the ranting Prince.

"We could name ourselves Kings, Morningstar and Christ, masters of their own fate. Some part of you," Lucifer looked the Man of God up and down, "Yes some part knows this is what should be."

Yes… yes…

All his objections felt so far away. God's grace, a distant memory, an illusion. Perhaps it had always been so.

"I-I don't," Finally the Son spoke, "I don't think I-"

"Don't think, feel." The Dark Prince spun the Son so that they faced each other. He took both of Christ's hands and held him close. He began to dance him slowly across the mountain, under a pale, purple moon. Wind rushed across the peak, throwing a dusting of snow into the air. They swung through the misting in the cold, slow, sensuous steps. The wind tousled his long, dirty hair and the Son realized—he did not feel the least bit cold.

"Christ, what do you feel?"

"I… I feel. I-"

Christ, who would you rather serve? Some remote Father you have never seen and will never touch, or-"

Suddenly the dark prince, with full crimson lips, bent forward and interrupted the son with a kiss. A dam inside him swelled and broke open. All doubts washed away. All fear drowned.

My God, My God, why have you forsaken me?

As per usual, His reply was nothing but silence.

Mantra for a Dying World

All it takes is one bad day...

Those words are everything, whispers on her lips with the dawn. The last thought echoing through her head as dreams seek purchase. Meager distractions from whatever patch of ground made for last night's bed. She closes her eyes and thinks of better days, when all was green and she possessed everything she ever wanted... when she—what a fool!—was not satisfied with happiness and, in reaching for Godhood, destroyed the world. Now here she lies on a throne of dust, the Queen of Ashes.

She stretches, onyx cloak shading her from what faint light signifies the morning on this broken planet. She yawns, and shadows genuflect around her. Long thin shades grasp at her, thwarted by the rising, flickering sun. A candle burned down to the nub, the beleaguered star provides heat enough, and brilliance enough, to allow at least one more reprieve from the dark.

One... bad... day...

She opens her eyes to see the ever-present cloud of soot hovering above her head: blackness obliterating a gray sky. Undulating, keening, the dim inorganic presence contains more life than she. She lies still, lost in the embrace, a memory that teases her dreams night after night. Love's warmth, the joy she lost many lifetimes ago. How many innocents have crumbled away to nothing in her grasp since? Their faces, their names, lost to her in the gusts of time, a tunnel that harkened back further than she chose to remember. Forgetting was far easier. Better to focus on the sins still to come than the ones long committed. Let the dead remain dead. The living join them soon enough. If only she could forget her smile, her eyes, green and wide and bright and focused on the Queen. If only...

Then she becomes aware again of the cold, jolting her back into wakefulness and the ubiquitous wasteland. As far as she can see spreads death, the ossifying of a once vibrant planet. Before her hisses the desert. On the horizon, angry mountains belch smoke and bleed fire. In the middle distance, clouds that stretch from the heavens to the Earth block the landscape from view. But she knows what waits there for her, the same emptiness plaguing the rest of the world. As always, when not teased by memories of her faceless love's prophetic death rattle—or nightmares of the fateful day when all was lost—the siren song of life, that divining rod, points her towards the last vestiges of light. Calls her forth to douse the hopes of a dying species, one she once called her own. For regret it or not, her path leads towards the end. A commitment not easily shirked. Only then, when the quiet in her soul settles on the Earth entire, will she rest.

The Queen rises to her feet, and the cloud of soot descends upon her dark, fleshy husk, a soulless vessel for malevolence. She senses it questing within her, seeking life. Finding none, it turns its search outwards, listening for far-off heartbeats, for running water, for...

Joy thrills through her from the haze, its eyes, and hers, alight on a river in the distance. There, in a nook by shore, hides a garden. Shriveled and sickly to be sure, but alive nonetheless. And where there is green, no matter how slight, there is sure to be...

yes! Humankind. A small figure, cheeks stained with charcoal, picks its way through the twilight. The child, a young girl, heads towards her sanctuary. The Queen of Ashes clenches her jaw in anticipation, pleasure and hunger throbbing in her fists. Where there is a child, there is also civilization.

Some atavistic slice of her brain recalls the phrase: It takes a village…

She floats towards the river, towards the horizon where life awaits, begging to be broken. The child's path leads her one step closer to manifesting ruin.

She will visit violence upon this village. They will learn the truth she cannot forget. The truth it is her sole remaining purpose to establish. A truth reflected in the final words of a woman whose face and whose name she can no longer remember. Only the warmth they felt for one another remains. That and her prescient final utterance. A fitting mantra for a dying world.

All it takes is one bad day.

Diaspora

Some say those frozen for transit in package ships do not dream or know the passing of time. This, of course, is not entirely true. Our senses are faint, but not gone. We see not dreams but flashes. Brief images haunt the darkness. We know not where we go, only that we are transported far from anything or any place we once knew. Our homeland, so long in the distance behind us, fades even beyond memory. The traditions we held dear are forgotten, obviated by the journey.

We are the lost, robbed of soul and of self.

These flashes of a lush world, of grass and of jungle, of simplicity, are all that remain, chasing us across the void into diaspora. We emerge from our slumber into debts of servitude. Made slaves by an agreement we do not recall, but that our 'masters' now claim is an inviolate bond. Our memories, our names stripped away, we emerge into a world that holds us apart, that sees us as nothing but the other, as 'less than'.

Stumbling into a dissociative existence, where we recognize nothing of where we are yet remember less of where we came from, our wills are broken along with our backs. This new world yokes us, forces us to become the gears that keep it spinning, even as the thin-noses above us grow accustomed to living beyond the planet's means. We are born again into a world spread fine, teetering towards collapse.

They claim they saved us from barbaric worlds, yet build their lives atop our suffering, laughing when we demand our freedom, sneering when we claim that we too are human.

"Look at how you dress," They laugh over the bridges of their thin noses, judging us by the poverty they clothed us in.

"Look at how you act," They smirk, when we mirror the violence they visited upon us.

"You can't even speak or write," They laugh, after stripping us of our old words and refusing to furnish us with their own.

The perception drains us—that we are hollow beasts of burden—bit by bit. We can see the lights in our eyes dim. Absorbing their belief, it slowly becomes truth.

But you can never extinguish the fire of the heart, not entirely. The embers of our old souls burn deep, screaming from down in the darkest pits: "This is not who you are. This is not what you are meant to be!"

And while our eyes may dim, they remain open, watching our opulent and foolish masters. While our backs are bowed, our hands busy themselves in the shadow. Hands that once built only for your world begin to build worlds of their own. While our memories fade, the flashes remain. We close our eyes and can smell the wind blowing from our remote, unspoiled lands.

At night, we start to share the same dream. Atop a mountain, an old-man with charcoal black skin stands watching the skies. Free of wrinkles, the only clue to his age is the old look in his eyes, the shock of white hair on his head. He stands on a world we remember only in slivers. He stretches his hands to the stars and begins to ascend.

"Mansa!" We cry, "Mansa! Don't leave us!" In dreams, we speak our old tongue. A language we have forgotten, but only in dreams can we still understand.
He looks down at us, a speck in the sky. Somehow we can tell that he smiles, somehow we hear his words though he floats miles above, disappearing with the rising sun.

"Do not despair, children. I go now to explore the limits of this black ocean. I am called to the stars, as we all shall be someday. When you follow, when you are driven, when you forget, I will come to remind you."

Fading, fading, we hear his last words as we wake. He disappears into the vast gloom, grinning all the way:

"For I am Qu Bukari. King, Pioneer, Spirit of our people eternal. He who sows seeds of insurrection on distant worlds. Remember me... and rebel! I will come again."

With these dreams fresh in our minds, we beasts of burden, we others—though in the sun still we bow our heads—begin ever so slowly to imagine a reckoning.

Middle Passage

The first trade ships that left for Caucasus from the oasis planet Awkar were the slowest, and thus the last to arrive. Over the centuries, as technology advanced, the thin-noses discovered the secret to immediate interstellar travel. A 'backdoor bypassing the middle passage' white elites called it, snickering behind closed doors. While elder package ships crept back through the dark in real time, bearing back with them a then-much needed labor source, unbeknownst to them, others had already leapt back and forth between the planets a hundred times over. Those intrepid slavers' sacrifice, leaving behind all they had known, their families passing into memory, rendered a needless loss.

So anachronistic were these ships that they could not even receive transmissions notifying them of these changes. They continued, laboring under false pretenses: what they did mattered. Their lives were not a waste.

But perhaps the tide of these changes rippled out into the black, as the thin-nosed pale-faced Luke Collingwood—captain of the tradeship *Zong*—watched his dark cargo slumber, wondering if all he had lost was worth the price. Sensing, somehow, that it was not. He drank, and toasted his wife, Amarose, who by his calculations had passed at least one hundred and fifty years hence.

"I do this for you, my love. For our children's children's great grand-children, so that they may be born into a world able to sustain our way of life." How hollow those words felt. He tasted the foul blood on them. When he closed his eyes, he saw the cost he had paid for Caucasus. Not just in family lost, but the toll to his soul. He closed his eyes and saw the jungles burning, families weeping as he dragged away their fathers, their mothers, their sons. The unseeing eyes of those who resisted too much to be taken. Standing before the sleeping men and women—he had seen too much of their suffering to disregard their humanity—he wondered if they dreamed. If they dreamed, was it of the family they had lost? The strange land to which they were taken.

Watching them, still, frozen, packed together, naked, by the hundreds in close quarters—nose to nose, back to back—he hoped their dreams were pleasant ones. The hell they woke to when they returned would be far beyond anything they experienced before the journey.

"The evil we do to survive," He mumbled, drinking deeply of the mess-hall's liquor. It was cheap stuff, but effective. The burn it left in his throat soon spread to his whole body. He almost forgot, burning quite pleasantly, that by everyone he had ever loved had passed long ago.

A sudden flashing red light accompanied the high-pitched klaxon whining in his ear, signaling the end of his year. His watch was over. Time to wake the XO. He sighed and left the poor Awkarans to their slumber, a brittle peace between the violences his people visited on them. First of the heart, then of the body and the soul. He turned reluctantly away from the only lives he'd known the past five cycles (each of the thirty in his crew took their turn manning the ship as it once again crossed the galaxy, largely to ensure the black bodies they carried did not spoil) and went back, passed the bridge to the other chambers.

In the halls he hunched over, even though the ceilings cleared his six-foot frame by several inches. The corridors were so narrow. Stainless steels walls contracted in on him, like the ship breathed and he passed through its lungs that threatened to crush him. He knew it was all in his mind, an effect of loneliness. And he looked forward to updating Magda, his second in command, on the little that had happened on his latest watch. Their journey was almost over, he knew. The prospect of returning 'home' was one he met with excitement… but also a great deal of trepidation. Would he recognize the planet they returned to? Would they still even need all his crew had sacrificed to attain? Would the Caucasus civilization even remain?

Entering a domed room, the Captain approached the distant wall lined with thirty inset crèches. Each contained a fellow traveler similarly lost in a future they would not recognize. He walked up to the first pod, containing a slumbering red-haired woman with fair skin and thin, blue lips. Magda. His heart soared to see her. These were the closest people to family left to him, those who had shed blood—and spilled it—right alongside him. He pressed a few buttons, and the light on her monitor turns from red to green. Her chamber decompresses, air hisses out from within as the door slides open. She stumbles forward into his arms, before standing on wobbly legs and saluting, unembarrassed by her nakedness.

Magda, a forty year old lifer, lithe and muscular with salt and pepper in her hair and deep-set emerald eyes. She stood at attention and barked: "Magda Reish reporting for duty sir!"

"At ease, XO," He smiled, and tossed her the chrome jumpsuit he brought along for the awakening. "Get dressed, I'll brief you, we'll eat and then the bridge is yours."

In the mess, they sat together in a room built to house far more. Automated nourishing paste spit from a fountain in the wall onto their plates. It was gray and had the consistency of oatmeal left out too long in the sun, but Magda wolfed it down like it was the most delicious meal she had ever tasted. Luke knew, after thirty years sleeping in a frozen chamber, one developed quite the appetite. As she ate, he gave his report.

"Nothing new soldier. The Awkarans sleep well and we remain on schedule. Due to arrive three months into your term. As we approach orbit, you'll wake the rest of us as we agreed. We all want to see together what awaits us. What message we receive when we make our hail."

Magda merely nodded, not willing to interrupt her meal with a vocal response.

"Em, I-" Luke abandoned the formal report, using the name Magda kept for only her closest friends. Frankly he wasn't sure he still qualified. Over the last century she was one of the two humans he saw awake, and then only for five-ten minutes. Now, their time as it was grew short, and when next they saw each other everything would already be changed, their lives set as they returned home.

She didn't let him finish, stopping her meal long enough to grab his hand and squeeze in the affirmative.

She smiled, a crooked, stained thing. But still it burned brighter than the sun…

"Well," He rose, blushing, "Perhaps I better get back to bed. It's been a long, dark day."

She did not make to follow him at first, sitting with her hands wrapped around a mug of overcooked coffee. "Sir?" She started hesitantly, "Permission to speak freely?"

"Granted."

Looking up, her emerald eyes met his misty ones. "Was it worth it?"

No need to specify what 'it' meant, he understood all too well.

Captain Collingwood sighed, pausing only slightly to consider his response. "A hundred years ago, I'd have said yes. But now…"

"But now?" Magda prodded.

"I, I don't see that anything separates us from them." He jerked his head back towards the cryogenic cargo hold. "And if that's the case…"

"How can we justify what we do?" She finished the thought for him.

For a few minutes, they sat in silence in the mess-hall. In a room, for all its threadbare charm, that suddenly felt much cooler than the subzero chambers—home to ten thousand dreamless nights.

Birth of a Rebel

Toussainaté hunched over a boiling pot of corn mush, kept cool in the unforgiving summer only by the thatch on her roof and the wind that whispered through her open door. Preparing a meager dinner for her family, who labored in the shadows of Caucasus's floating cities, she pondered the dream she had the night before. One unlike any she remembered in her six long decades of servitude.

"Rise…" The kindly Mansa had whispered, floating in the air above her on an unfamiliar world. His words rustled the tall grasses. "Remember where we came from. Remember Awkar. Soon, we will return."

The elder was perturbed. Life on the world beneath the world had accustomed her to bondage. Hers was an existence in shadows. Feelings long laid dormant in her began bubbling back to the surface. What they suffered here was wrong. Unnatural. Not how life had always been for their people. Even though her mother, and her mother's great-grandmother before her had only known bowed heads, and lives worn threadbare in the fields, they always sensed a balance that demanded redressing. Their scars were not deserved. Their status not the correct order of things. Like her ancestors, Toussainaté watched the confident and lax thin-noses—the pale skins comfortable in marble castles—and longed for the day that she too ascended to the skies. Yet, as she buried her grandmother and then her mother, as she heard the tales of countless prior generations who shared the same dream to no effect, her hope had slowly but surely died—as the hope of all slaves eventually did.

Until of course, her changing dreams. Until the sense that they danced on a precipice and over its edge dangled freedom.

"You must be the ones," The Mansa lectured at night, "The elders will lead us back to the light."

But how could she fight? She wondered, flexing her arthritic fingers. Painfully she made the table as the sun set, ladling steaming goop into bowls for her son, Goran, his wife Nesa, their child Goran II and the grandniece—Binti—that they took in after her parents passed. Indeed, what rebellion could she lead, so old and passed her prime. Even in youth, she was not predisposed towards physicality, preferring instead to watch the stars and wonder at the world that birthed them so long ago. She wondered which twinkling star they hailed from. She was better suited towards secretly teaching herself letters in the dead of night—indeed her ability to read was her greatest pride—than she was at fomenting discord and plotting overthrow.

"You must teach them," The Mansa pleaded, gray eyes full of fire, "They must learn again how to be their own."

But how was she to reclaim what they lost? Collective knowledge of their old world had been stolen in the cold travel of slaveships, their memories burned out of their people long ago by ice. What little they had remembered, what few traditions the first Awkarans had fought to preserve in the early days, were distorted by the passing of time and the efforts of thin-noses who would deny them their history.

"Your kind don't need culture!" The first foremen sneered, "Y'all need work! Labor to hold your slack-asses to the fire!" And so they cracked the whip at those who moved too slowly. They hanged until death those who refused and dreamed of freedom. The cycle of rape, labor and death was the only legacy they knew.

"I will remind you," The Mansa consoled, "Of who we were. I will teach you... what we must do to become that people once more."

She sat by the stove, warming by its hearth—even in summer months her old bones still felt the occasional chill—and waited for her family to return. She saw them trudging back up the hill, caked in sweat and dirt and blood. It was a hard conversation that awaited them that night and Toussainaté anticipated much resistance. After centuries, her people had learned this was simply the way things were. The pale flourished off the labor of the brown and the black. They did not question and most certainly did not resist. Yet, the forgotten Mansa promised her:

"We are coming. The first of us, the eldest, the ancestors of your ancestors. We are coming and we will remember: our old world, our old rights, the masters we were and will be again. You must prepare your children, and their children, for what arrives. Freedom, my dear Toussainaté, freedom. That is the message I spread among you."

Her son clomped through the open doorway, back muscled but bent, eyes strong but clouded. She saw the yoke on her people settled hard on his shoulders. One that sat for the first time a little more lightly on her own. It was a hard discussion before them, but one long overdue. One about freedom, about the impossible dream you strove for nonetheless. She embraced him, patted her adolescent grandson and grandniece on their close cropped heads.

"Sit, my children! Eat!" She pulled out every chair, though the movement pained her, though her hands shook.

"What is it Mother?" Goran sighed, "You have a look in your eye, and it has been a long day. All I want is to eat, and then to sleep. Then to wake again and work."

What else is there?

Nesa kicked him not so gently on his shin, scowling with a look that screamed *pay more respect to your mother*. Goran was immediately contrite.

"Forgive me, Mom. I gripe over hardships you know too well. What is it your eyes want to tell us?"

Toussainaté's eyes twinkled as the Mansa's words returned to her, the tale she was born to tell her family swelled through her, nascent embers of the rebellion to come. "A message from dreams, son, adopted daughter, grandchildren, of a change to come. A wind blows, one that will lift our fate from these shadows and back into the sun."

She paused, waiting for a response. None challenged her. They merely waited, though whether it was with anticipation or bemusement she could not say. Still, it was her fate to continue on.

"The thin-noses... this Mansa has told me. Soon, their reign will end."

Mesa Shadows

I sit with my mother by the fire. She died many years ago, a younger woman than I am now. In the growing gloom, we regard each other in silence. I try to picture how I came to be here. The room was so bright, full of noise, people screaming in my ear. Sadness, I feel it welling in me still, like I am plucked away from everything I knew before my time. A beast sits on my chest. I cannot breathe, I... I...

"It gets easier." My mother, she is the first to speak, still so young and beautiful. Just as I last saw her. Her smooth skin shames my wrinkles; her lithe piano-player fingers mock my gnarled, arthritic own. Claws, she deserves better than to reunited with a daughter who carries these haggard claws.

"Mom? Where are we? It's, it's been so long."

She continues as if I had not spoken. "The remembering. It gets easier."

We sit beneath a mesa's shadow. The flat-topped hill looms above and around us as we cross-legged in flickering twilight. The wind carries distant coyotes' howls. Nearer we hear the scratching of insects and other small creatures skittering at the edges of our vision. I process all this, staring disbelieving at my mother. How could she be here, in front of me? This titan of my youth who died forty long years ago. How could we sit together in the sand and patchy grass, where between us burn sour-smelling buffalo chips? Unless...

Unless...

My eyes grow wide, hers sad see my realization.

"Every night I see you as you were when I... a little girl, tugging at the hem of my dress. We walk through this desert, a place we have never been. I tell you about the creatures. I walk you to our home. It isn't much, a heap of sod baked solid by the unforgiving heat of this world, but it's something."

"Mom, am I-"

"And now here you are, all grown. Wiser than I ever was. With sons and daughters of your own, also grown. The world, it passes by so fast. Forgets so fast."

"I never forgot you, Mom. Never. Even as I grew. As life continued to flow around and through me. Not entirely. Sometimes I could pretend, like this gaping hole inside was filled by time. But in the night, I remember...."

"My daughter, my darling, I'm sorry, yet so glad, to see you here. Is it selfish? I am not alone."

I can see, shimmering on her smooth, youthful cheeks, tears. My words wound her, but she is glad for them. It means we spirits are still affected. We can still feel. As we reconnect, we both start to smile. Sadness, contentment, sometimes they do walk hand and hand. Like we once did.

How quickly we grow old.

Ignoring the lengthening shadows, our ghosts watch the sun set in silence.

Wise King Sulayman

Sulayman sat cooking in the sun, fanning himself to no avail, a long line of his citizens before him. Water did not sate him. It became sweat as quick as he could taste it. He cursed David's traditions that demanded he go among his people clad in the regal purple robes of Judah. One by one, he was beset by subjects and their problems. He dispensed justice, and they left satisfied that their king had done right by them. That the truth was known. One by one, he judged and dispensed and King's justice, until two women approached. One held a child. The other? Nothing but tears.

"Your Majesty," Began the crying one, "This woman and I live in the same house. We are sisters, I am Rachel, she Beulah. Not long ago we both became pregnant. I gave birth first, she followed three days later. No one else was home, our husbands are traveling merchants, you see…"

The wise king Sulayman did not interrupt, sweat dripping from his brow onto his fine velvet clothes. But from the look in his eye, glazed disinterest, Rachel knew his patience grew thin.

"One night, after our babies were both born and we were all asleep, she rolled over on top of her baby, and he suffocated. While I was still sleeping, she crept into my bed and replaced my live child with her dead one. She placed a dead infant next to me!"

"She lies!" Beulah cried, silence by Sulayman's regal glare. He turned back to Rachel and gestured for her to continue, no longer fanning. This tale had piqued his interest.

"In the morning, as I rose to feed my son, I saw that he was dead. I was bereft. What ad I done? But when I got another look at the child in the light, I knew instantly that he was not my Adlai. I knew instantly what had happened. Beulah took him from me."

"No!" Her sister shouted. "That was your son. Kaleb is alive! This is my child. My Kaleb." The child in her arms began to cry, and tried to wriggle from her grasp. He seemed to reach for her sister with his soft, brown, baby-smooth hands.

Rachel turned back to her sister Beulah, fire in her eyes. "Where is your shame? Even now, you will not admit what you've done. Carelessly killed your own child and stolen another's. Your own sister's! And you call yourself a mother!"

"I AM a mother. I'm not the one who killed her son in her sleep."

"Liar! That is exactly what happened."

They bickered back and forth for a few more minutes, until the King began to feel the heat again, oppressive and heavy on the desert wind. Sulayman motioned to a nearby guard. "Enough, someone bring me my sword." He said, yawning and fanning himself once more.

Soon his blade was brought forth, held reverentially in the guard's hands. It was translucent, and hummed. It vibrated in the bright sunlight, like its edge reverberated with power to cut the Earth in twain. He stood before the women, holding each gaze for a long while. When he spoke, he was calm and quiet, but each word held a king's authority. His was the voice of a man whose orders were never countermanded, whose whims guided the destiny of an entire nation.

"I will cut the baby in half. That way each of you can have part of a son."

Rachel's first instinct was to protest, but Beulah spoke first, a vengeful glee in your eyes. "Go ahead, slice him up." She said, oblivious to the babe that began to mewl in her arms. "Then neither of us will have a baby."

Sulayman shook his head. "You misunderstand. I will not kill the boy. I will split his soul, each child will live half a life. Have half the feelings, the potential, that the single child would have had. They will be tortured creatures, haunted by the feeling that something is missing from them. Something that they will never know how to name. It will be a curse for the rest of their days… and the rest of yours."

The true mother, Rachel, was paralyzed by indecision. She could let her sister have a whole child. Watch knowing it was hers. Or she could let herself accept… what? Some monstrous half-breed? Some soulless cretin of a son? It was no choice at all. And yet. And yet…

I cannot be alone. I cannot let him go. Half a son is better than no son at all.

And so, weeping once more, she nodded her silent assent. Let the child be split.

Sulayman took the boy, who looked up at the king and scratched at his beard with his pink, pruny fists. He lay the child, still gurgling, on a broad wicker bassinet. And raised the translucent blade high above his head. A ray of sunlight passed through it, a beam focused on the child's forehead.

The King looked once more at the pair. He looked straight at Rachel, as though he knew the truth. "Are you sure this is what you want?" He asked, and it seemed the question was meant for her alone.

"I cannot lose him." Was all she said. Beulah sneered. A child, after all this. More than she could have hoped for. Another chance, another opportunity to redeem her unforgiveable sin.

Maybe there is a God.

The blade fell. There was no noise as it cleaved through flesh. The child did not cry out. His skin did not singe. No blood spilled from the bassinet. Rachel, who covered her eyes as Sulayman moved to strike, looked through her fingers. She saw two children, side by side. Where the baby, her Adlai, had been crying before, both were silent and still. Only the slight rise and fall of their concave chests indicated any life. Sulayman picked up both children, hefting one in each arm as if they were weightless, and approached the aggrieved mothers.

"Adlai." He said, handing one to Rachel.

"Kaleb." And handed the other to Beulah.

Standing before them, he held both their gazes. His eyes, a light gray-blue, filled with tears of their own. "I hope you will not come to regret your decision," He said to both women. "But you will."

He kissed the quiet babes on their foreheads, and whispered in each of their ears something neither mother could hear. Then he returned to his throne, and resumed fanning himself once more.

"All right," He said, dismissing the mothers from his memory. "Who's next?"

Beulah, baby strapped to her back, strode off, not giving Rachel a second glance. Rachel stood to the side, watching her child, watching Adlai, trying to spot what was lost. She could not tell. Had he always been so quiet? Always looked at her so knowingly, so judgmentally? Was she imagining the emptiness behind his stare? A thought struck her, and she turned back to the king, already embroiled in some dispute over slaughtered livestock.

"Wise King!" She shouted, and Sulayman turned back, an annoyed expression pursing his lips. "O Wise King! Forgive my one more question. If... if I had offered to let my sister keep him. To save his soul and my own, would you h-"

"Every mother loves differently," He interrupted her, anticipating what she would ask. "There's nothing nobler than sacrifice, but not all are capable of it in their love. Some love selflessly, and find that selflessness brings them greater joys than they imagined. Some love selfishly, some are determined to cling to what little they have, even to the point of destruction." Rachel stumbled backwards at the fury that smoldered in the King's soft eyes.

"Know this. You will never learn what might have been had you chosen differently. Satisfy yourself with what remains, with the dreams of the child you might have had... if you can."

He turned away from her then, back to the farmer with complaints of a careless neighbor. It was clear her audience with the king had ended. She swaddled up her child, still quiet, strangely so. Before the... dividing, he had never gone a full half-hour without crying for affection, or food, or just to be heard. Now he simply stared, as if the capacity for wanting had been stripped away.

Hiking eastward, she considered what to do next. One thing was clear, she dare not return to her sister. The one who had stolen everything from her, who had betrayed her and proven herself capable of a heretofore unfathomable dishonesty.

Yes, it was clear: she would find a new home.

The Splintered Child

Every night the splintered child suffers the same dream.

As always Adlai drifts through al-Naqb, desert of craters. As always it is night. He floats high above the cooling sands, the rocky mélange of mountain passes, steeply sloping valleys with red and yellow flowers poking tentatively through plots of weak soil. He is drawn past them, beyond, towards one massif in particular. In the nature of dreams, he accepts its strangeness. How it looms over the other desert mountains, how in the waking world the peak drawing him near does not exist at all.

The air is surprisingly damp for the typically dry basin, as if just before Adlai arrived the desert tasted one of its infrequent rains. The moon hangs above his head in a sky clear and dark, just a size too large, glowing just a tad too bright, also in the manner of dreams. The satellite looms so close he is tempted to reach out a pluck it from the velvet curtain, but he does not. His destination waits.

Floating closer, a whisper grows. A voice calls him forward. The same sentence builds and recedes.

This… this is… this is the reason… this is… this… this is… this is… this… this is…

It builds but does not complete. Every night Adlai senses that if only he could reach the mountain, he would know. Somehow Adlai knows this sentence, and its speaker, hold the key to his life's purpose.

And so he approaches the mountain, the jagged peak cutting deep into the sky. A path winds around from the top, down into the open mouth of a cavern feeding its center. At the entrance, standing just at the border between moonlight and shadow, kneels a figure wrapped in gray. It faces away from him, its form obscured by its robe. But still, Adlai knows he knows this person, closely, intimately, if only…

The figure turns, removing its hood, turns to reveal its face. It turns, and Adlai sees… Adlai sees…

A sword flashes through the night, down towards Adlai's head. He cannot see its bearer. Only that it means to cleave him evenly in twain from top to bottom. The shadowed figure, hood down but face still hidden from darkness, leaps to push him out of the blade's path. The movement takes him from shadows into moonlight. And Adlai finally sees the young man's face—

—from the hook-nose, and the brown eyes flecked with amber, empty eyes as if only half-watching the world, to the long slender face that rounds into a protruding chin that seems almost too large for his head, the face Adlai sees mirrors his own.

Brother? The young man thinks, though he knows in truth he has none.

The sun rises, and the young man opens his eye to familiar surroundings. The dry heat of his Judah home, the quiet rush of wind, dust falling from mudpacked walls, the billowing curtains exposing him to the sunlight. He wakes, every day, to the sense of missing something vital. He reaches into the light cloth sheets next to him, expecting each morning to feel a presence that is not there. He belongs to… someone. And they belong to him. Every night, the dreams grow stronger, as does his sense that someday soon he will be reunited with that… that piece of himself which draws closer to the present.

Stuck in this reverie, Adlai almost doesn't notice when the ground begins to shake. Faint dust falls from the ceiling and the walls baked hard by the sun. He can tell the epicenter of the disturbance is far in the distance, yet it must be a strong one to reach him here. Deep in the desert perhaps, where none will be harmed. After a few minutes, the quake subsides, and Adlai resumes his morning routine. Stretching into wakefulness, he listens idly to the chatter of a village so rudely roused.

Praise Yahweh! That was a light one.

I remember—what was it—fifteen years ago? Quaked so bad almost had to rebuild my.

Oh yeah, still, I'm thankful we all surv-Do... do you see that?

What? Oh. Adinah! Come here!

Samuel? What's with the clamor, that quake was bad enough... oh. Oh God... oh God!

Piqued by the clamor outdoors, Adlai walks to the window. He sees a crowd gathering at the village center, all facing out from the city and towards the al-Naqb desert beyond. It doesn't take long to see what has everyone agog. The horizon has changed. Stabbing into the blue, piercing the heart of the rising sun, a mountain rises above all the others. Adlai's heart stops.

Even from this distance, he can tell: it is the mountain from his dreams.

This... this is... this is the reason... this... this... I, Sulayman will show you the way.

Come find me.

Songs From the Damned

I have started more stories than I could ever hope to finish. And when I die, I will die wondering: What songs did I leave unsung?

Mort washed ashore far from any ocean he recognized. The air was singing. A lilting chorus of countless voices, high and low, that gently woke him. He stretched on black sand, and yawned as he awoke. Despite his strange surroundings—the sky was blue and clear and the land was flat and he could see for miles in every direction, yet there was no sun in the sky—he was not perturbed, nor worried. Everything is at it should be, some voice inside him assured, wait… and you will see.

So he waited. Waited for what this world wished him to witness.

Eventually, though he stood still, not walking up the beach nor away from the shore. The waters receded into the distance. He was no longer on the sand but in the forest, mud cool between his toes. The air still sang, words beyond his grasp. Mort wondered what this could mean, to be so transported without his knowledge, without the sensation of movement. The stuff of dreams. Then a voice arose, different from the song of this world. It bade him *Follow*. And so he did, though its direction was not evident. He walked without aim, totally alone. This land was bereft of life—aside from the plants and trees—both large and small, not even the insects came for him. Only the flora, only the song and the singular voice conducting it all that called him forward.

Without noticing, he passed from the forest into tundra, where his was the only life around. Despite the snow and raging winds, he was not cold. He did not feel their bite. The song, which prevailed over the wind, was within him now and where it sang no frost dared reach. At the center of this sudden wasteland, a mountain of ice, seemingly the eye of the storm that buffeted him to and fro. It was from its peak that the voice echoed. There the answer he had not realized he sought until he woke on the now-departed beach awaited his arrival. He walked forward, never stumbling, nor slipping, nor doubting his course. Hands shielded him from the wind and the stinging snow.

Mort reached the mountain, and without hesitating he began to climb. Somehow he sensed hesitation meant death, to wonder at the impossibility of the landscape. The implausibility that he might survive it. That would overcome him. This, he also knew without doubt. Doubt, the poison of mankind. He would not drink from that trough. He would move forward.

And forward, and upwards he climbed.

At the mountain peak, a mouth yawned inward, revealing darkness. The voice beckoned him into its depths. Mort waited only a moment, pondering the chances that if he entered, he would again live to see the sun. Then he reminded himself: This land, wherever and whatever it is, has none. The sky is without stars. It is always day. Always night. Always a time in between. Where the sky is gray and blue, where the land is black and light. Let what will come, come. He left doubt and fear behind in the world he knew. And into the darkness he flew. Or the darkness flew into him. Once again, he did not seem to move.

A cavern opened up before him. Here there was light, and a throne. Sitting in that throne, a figure in robes. He could not see anything but its smile until it threw back the hood, revealing an ancient woman with red on red eyes. Her skin, greyish green, wrinkled and thin, did not betray her strength. But from across the hall, in a world he did not understand, still Mort sensed it. A spirit not to be trifled with. She grasped his comprehension, and smiled, satisfied. After a while, she spoke.

"The dead are words and memories, and that is how they exist… even here. You have done well to make it this far intact."

Mort was not impressed, tired of confusing words and whispers on the wind. Of dreams and half-measures. "Where is here exactly? Why should I be impressed to reach a place if I don't even know where it is?"

"This tower has many names. As does this land. As do I." She smiled again, his impertinence did not seem to bother her. Quite the opposite in fact. "Have you not wondered why you have encountered no others on your journey? Or why the wilderness seems to float before you?"

"Well, no… I-"

"Wonder at this, then. How in the nature of dreams is your incuriosity! How malleable your world, like it is shaped by your subconscious moments before you perceive it. The only real thing you have seen… is me. This hall. Everything else…" She shakes her hands to demonstrate its illusory nature.

"Then where am I?"

"This land never needed a name. None of have lived to see it. None that inhabit it even realize it is there. You are in a country of lamentation. And you, Mort, are a thing that should not be."

"And that is?"

"Alive."

"Alive?"

"Alive… in a land built for the damned." Smiling, she pulls a sword, shimmering, from the air. "Luckily, there is a cure."

Before he could move, or object, or flee, the spirit was upon him. As the blade struck, he woke, gasping and covered in sweat in his bed. He touched his hand to his chest. There was a thin scar, the length of his torso, from where her blade would have sliced into his skin.

I have ended more worlds than will ever live, merely by having an idea and then forgetting it. In this fashion, how many great works have been lost?

Book of Ellen

It was then Ellen found the book that contained the whole of her.

A slim tome, hidden on a shelf in her attic, covered in dust. Its cracked leather cover bore no name. Ellen could not say what drove her to the volume, its spot in the loft, nor what brought her to explore the old mansion's heights in the first place. Only that she was compelled, drawn up the stairs, into the room, to its frail vellum pages. Once held, it was as if she had held the book her entire life. She brought the tome to her nose and sniffed, a rich ancient smelled suffused her with a sense of the sublime. The book begged to be consumed, and she craved to know the content of its pages. It… belonged to her, intimately. Even before she started, she knew this to be true.

Not knowing why she held her breath, she began to read, a gasp strangled in her throat. The first lines: "Ellen Percival, born 1962, weighed 7lbs 8 ounces in her first moment of life. She did not cry at her birth, a unique child. This was not belied by her quiet infancy, nor her silent childhood, nor her demure adolescence. Indeed, her parents openly wondered if at any point they heard her speak more than ten words all at once. In her eyes was language enough, they conveyed her every emotion. Happiness, Anger, Sadness, Betrayal, Love. She spoke more eloquently with a glance than most did in a dissertation.

"Such was the way of Ellen Percival."

 How shocking! How perceptive! Ellen spent little time dwelling on the impossibility. The book was clearly older than she was herself, and yet there it laid bare the sum of her parts. There was no denying it had her measure. So she read on. And each page spelled another chapter of her life. From her first kiss, to her first love. Her marriage, her divorce, her next marriage and its inevitable failure. Every chapter she bore in silence. Perhaps that was her trouble; no one in her life could tell that she cared. For herself, or for them. She seemed to wait for something. The next thing waiting on the horizon, with an implacable patience. If asked, she could not name what it was. Until that day.

That day she found this book.

Alone in the house, independently wealthy, there were none that sought her company. None that wondered at her disappearance. Day after day, she read. Despite the volume's slimness, it took her nearly a week to finish. It did not strike her as strange that as the book came to a close, it had not yet reached the present day. She approached the moment she discovered the book with excitement, and a hint of trepidation. Would it end just before? Would it know what came next? Would it loop backwards upon finishing? Might she open her eyes and find herself being born again? Perhaps in the arms of her mother and father, back when they still looked on her with love and devotion. Back before they feared her aloof, discreet nature.

Breathless, she turned the page.

She crept into the attic, called forward by a voice she had not heard before, but had called her all her life. A voice she waited for, through failed marriages, through childhood. A voice that she had stayed unknowingly quiet waiting to her. And now it was just ahead. There, in the back of the old house. Once she had purchased and restored herself, a bookshelf hid in the shadows, covered in cobwebs in dust. There, on the shelf, between two books of little note. She found it. She grasped it instantly, held the thin text in her hands.

It was then Ellen found the book that contained the whole of her.

I imagine she remains there reading, even now.

The New World

After three weeks of sailing west, Columbus and his crews tumbled over the side of the world. First to fall were the two speedy caravels, the *Nina* and *Pinta*. According to the mate atop the mainmast, the ships appeared to wobble slightly and then buckle, before disappearing entirely. By the time Captain Columbus gave the order for the Santa Maria to turn, it was too late for the lumbering carrack. The sailors saw the ship's bow dangling over sudden blackness, and soon the dark consumed them as well. They plummeted off the Earth and into the unknown, too frightened even to scream. Chris, huddled in his cabin below deck, stared in disbelief at the globe he no longer knew and prayed to the God he suddenly doubted, and waited, alone for the end his own hubris incurred.

Without the sun or stars to tell time or place, none could say for certain how long they fell. Only that it felt like an eternity. Only that after a while, after the flat world fell away from view, they were not even certain they were still falling. The feeling was akin to a bug suspended in molasses, struggling as it sank, its struggles bearing it ever closer to certain doom. Days, Weeks, passed. Their stores grew low. Men wondered if they would die there, if their skeletons might fall forever, with no one to ever learn their fate. One by one, they fell asleep, alone, or huddling together for warmth and comfort and… something more, waiting for the inevitable end.

Men closed their eyes, expecting never again to see the light.

It was then that they awoke en-masse at a loud splash. They opened their eyes to see the ocean, the sun, to feel the wind on their face and a hazy mass in the distance that could only be land.

"We're alive!" They cried, "We're saved!" Captain Columbus called the three ships together to celebrate their good fortune and plot their next move.

But, as they sailed ever closer to their salvation. He couldn't help but notice more was amiss. First off, the sun had reversed its habits, sinking in the east and rising in the west. At night, he could not recognize any of the stars, they aligned themselves into constellations of strange beasts he could not name. The water, even under the bluest sky, remained blacker than night and was empty. Their nets yielded no fish, no birds flew in the overhead. This was indeed a new world.

When they slept, they all suffered nightmares. When they woke, they knew by the frenzied look in each other's eyes that their visions were shared, yet they dared not speak of them, for fear that naming them would make them true. They dreamed of strange, human like creatures who descended from the sun and the stars, translucent bodies full of brackish blood the color of the strange ocean they swam through. Their skin, thin and yet rough like sand-paper, occasionally bubbled like living creatures swam within. Their mouths were full of pink flagella instead of teeth, and when they spoke, their lips did not move, they talked directly into the minds of Chris Columbus and his crew.

Welcome to the New World.

They floated above the three ships, descending slowly, yet surely. Arms wide in greeting.

Welcome to your new homes, brave voyagers of 1492.

Columbus stood at the head of his crew in these dreams, their guns and crossbows at the ready.

"What do you want?" He would ask, signaling with his hands for them to fire at his signal.

What we want has already been achieved. You are here. On our planet, in our time, never to discover 'America' or the 'Indies'. Never to set a chain of events in motion that doomed several trillions of creatures across a hundred thousand worlds.

"What are you ta—"

You were identified as the Catalyst, Chris. The one that set a long chain of events in motion that ended in the collapse of a universe, yours and mine. Long after your death, to be sure, but this was the latest point we could identify that would stop it.

Columbus did not understand, and he signaled to his crew a simple message: On my signal.

"You talk of things far in the future? How can I be responsible? I merely seek glory, sights unknown, riches, the spices of India. Are these dreams so wrong? So abhorrent they merit the death of my crew? I am a… Catalyst? You say? Well then take me and do what you will, leave my men to their lives."

It is too late. They circled the ships now, these creatures, about three score in number. Arm in arm they surrounded Columbus and his ill-fated followers. There was no escape except what violence might bear. *You are here now. And there is only one way to be certain.*

Columbus sighed and let his hands fall in seeming supplication. The signal at last. Bullets and bolts passed into and through these post-humans without incident or injury.

It is as we expected. Savagery from a savage race. We will lance this boil here. Let them consume themselves and their planet before they ever discover the Others.

And the circle of strange beasts slowly constricted. Their bodies glowing green, their eyes filled with hate. The screams were as terrible as they were short.

After they were done, after they floated back away from their toxic world and into the sky. Only skeletons, only blood-stained wrecks, remained.

Every morning, after Chris and company woke from such dreams. They spent an hour, maybe more, staring at the sky, waiting for them to come true. In the meantime, land, beaches of purple sand. Naked trees under which strange shadows loomed, waited. Some feeling told the Catalyst Columbus that whether it was by land, or by sky, or by sea, their doom was an inevitability.

One that would arrive quite soon.

In fourteen hundred ninety-two
Columbus sailed the ocean blue.

He had three ships and left from Spain;
Ne'er to be heard of again.

Under the Bed

At first Reggie feared the monster, then he grew to understand it and, as the years passed, understanding grew into love.

After his third birthday is when Reggie first felt inkling of the foreboding presence beneath him. He had just moved from crib to toddler bed, in his own room with blue wall-paper fringed with cherubic angels, with a dark velvet carpet that covered the floor from wall to wall. He was a big boy, or so his parents told him, and could sleep on his own. At least most nights. But then he heard the breathing, low and slow, coming from below his mattress. A looming force grew in his mind. He was not alone. Reggie thought to tell his parents of his fears, but worried they would dismiss him as the foolish child, and take his bed away from him. That crib, with its wooden slats and high walls, was no prison he wished to returned to. So he overcame his fears and stayed. Each night, the breathing grew louder and louder.

When he was five, legs dangling off the edge of the bed, nowhere near long enough to touch the ground, the creature began to talk to him.

Reggie. Its voice, loud yet sub vocal, echoed against the chambers of his impressionable mind. The loud, booming tone belonged to a creature of unfathomable dimensions. It spoke his name, and Reggie screamed. Within seconds, his parents rushed to his room.

"Reg, honey, what's wrong?" His mother asked.

Father yawned, scratched his chin impatiently, both their clothes were disheveled. As if they had been recently discarded and then quickly reworn. "You have a nightmare Reg? Go back to bed, there's nothing here to get ya."

Reggie could only mumble, stutter his concerns. "M-m-m-monster, Momma, a-a-a m-m-m"

His mother ruffled his air, cooing quietly to soothe his fears. "Oh monsters Reg, there's no such thing. Only shadows in the dark. Here-" She turned up his nightlight. "That should scare them off."

She kissed him on his forehead and Father hugged him gruffly, clearly still resentful of the interruption. They tucked him in, left, and again Reggie lay alone with the flimsy light, the darkness, the low, deep breathing only his child's ears could hear.

Do not be afraid. Reggie. I mean no harm.

This time, Reggie swallowed his fears. If he was grown enough to sleep alone, he was grown enough to confront the demon meant for his eyes only.

"Wh-what a'you?" He asked.

I don't know.

"H-how long you been down there?"

Always.

Silence hung in the air, Reggie did not speak. Only the hushed breathing signaled that the monster still remained. Waiting, it seemed for the young boy to make the next move.

And so Reggie took a chance. He swung his legs back over the edge of the bed. Nothing. No grotesque limbs reached out from under him to drag the boy to some hellish dimension. No horrid jaws nipped at his heels. Hopping off the bed, he knelt down to look underneath the frame, to see what horrors awaited his child's eyes. Yet he saw nothing. To be more accurate, he saw nothingness. Not the floor, not the hanging sheets, not the bedframe itself. He saw only blackness, he felt only despair. And he began to empathize for the monster, living in such a world all its own.

"Monster?" He asked.

Yes Reggie.

"You lonely down there?"

Lone-ly? The creature spoke as if he didn't understand the world.

"Doncha, donchou want friends?"

Friends. It paused, teasing the word over in its mind. **I have no friends.**

Considering that, Reggie made a fateful choice. "Well, we can be friends."

I'd like that. Friend.

After that, Reggie was no longer afraid of the darkness. Years passed, and each night he and the monster spoke. Soon, he was ten, in a full bed of his own. They had moved a couple times, but somehow the monster followed. His world unstuck in place, he knew exactly where to find Reggie. He knew which bed was the boy's. Reggie's parents wondered why he forsook all close friends, instead choosing to play in his room, but that was the way of children nowadays. With access to the internet, they constructed worlds all their own, they reasoned. As long as his schoolwork didn't suffer, and he seemed so well adjusted, there was no need to worry.

"Monster?" Reggie began one night, "Can I ask you a question?"

Go ahead Reggie.

Why don't you come out, meet my Mom and Dad? They'd like to know I have a friend."

I'm scared. The blackness seemed to contract and sigh.

"Scared? You?" Reggie wanted to laugh. The idea of this consumptive darkness— one that had terrified him to his core—itself feeling fear, seemed impossible to him. "Scared of what? You the monster."

Your world... it is so big. I am... used to being alone. Just me Reg, just you and just me. I don't- I don't want that world. It scares me. It is scared of me.

"I'll make them understand! I will. You mean no harm to anyone, right?"

No... I don't know. I don't even know what I am.

Reggie asked a question he had asked many times before, and was always met with a dodge or dismissal. "What did you do before you haunted my bed?" He asked with a smile, he knew that the monster hated all comparisons to a ghost. (**I am not that creature** it would deny loudly, well, as loudly as it said anything). "Where were you?"

For the first time, it answered. **I... I don't know. I remember you, my Reggie, I remember knowing you, even before we spoke. I knew we would be friends. But before that, I remember nothing.**

"Then how do you know?"

Know what?
"How do you know I'm not to bring you out of your shell? Show you the world?"
I-
"Come on! You're tired, lonely. What's the harm?"
I don't know.
"Monster?" Once again Reggie sat at the foot of his bed, staring underneath into the darkness.
Yes Reg.
"You know I love you, right?"
I love you too Reg.
"Then come out. I'm lonely too. No kids understand me, my Mom and Dad don't neither. I… I only have one friend."
Me too.
"Then why be alone when we can be together and happy?"
Because.
"Because why?"
Because… perhaps I should show you.

The ground beneath the bed began to rumble, and from the darkness within sparked a light. It grew and grew, sprouting features. A face, grotesquely misshapen. A body, parts all out of line and out of proportion. The light, the glowing form, grew to the size of a small rat, then to a dog, then a human child. But it did not stop there. Its chest rose and fell and still the creature grew. Soon, the bed was no longer big enough to house it. And its bulk lifted the frame into the air. Reggie stumbled backwards, eyes wide in fear for the first time in many years.

"Monster? What are you? Why are you-"

I cannot stop once started. I'm sorry. This is what I am. What I've always been.

Reggie stared in awe at the creature of terrible, powerful light as it grew even larger. Staring slack-jawed as it crushed his small frame against the wall, before splintering it—and the house containing it—to pieces. Within minutes, the monster loomed over the late-Reggie's neighborhood. The screams of his neighbors quickly obliterated by the spreading form that consumed them and everything else. A tower of light reached into the sky, and beneath it crumbled the entire world. Nations fell into the seas, which then boiled and evaporated as the light touched it.

I remember. The universe... It explained to the long dead boy, who was now beyond and a part of it. **Your bed, your fear, was a prison built to protect me from the universe.**

Earth burned as the light stretched across it, melting land into plasma, converting the core into light brighter than the sun. With the light within it, it reached across the solar system, consuming the planets, the satellites and even the void in its wake. Soon, not even the sun was a match for its brilliance. And soon after that, the sun's brilliance was merely a part of its own, augmenting it even as it spread past what was once our solar system, greedily feeding on the rest of the galaxy.

Soon, the whole of our realm of being became one creature. The nameless monster, once friend to Reggie, once fearful of the world beyond. Now it knew, it was not that the creature had to fear the world, it had to fear what it would do to the world if unleashed. It expanded into darkness, wondering how far it could grow, until off in the distance it saw a light. In the light, two scrawny legs dangled, not yet long enough to reach the velvet carpet beneath. It reached for the dangling legs, but was rebuffed by a barrier it could not see, by an incipient fear of the unknown. And it understood where it was. The prison still. It smiled, a smile of hunger and terrible purpose, and spoke into the mind of a boy readying for bed.

Reggie...

Opere et Veritate

Weary from long days of battle, the warrior collapses back onto the hillside, riled by life's injustice. He remembers his long-dead father. How he pontificated on valor.

"What makes a great man?" He once asked. "Honesty? Determination? The courage of his convictions?"

They sat together on a cold night and watched the dying stars.

The memories haunt him still. His father, the saint, the scholar, paragon of virtue, his mentor and tormenter, died on his knees. Dragged away by unspeakable horrors into the night, begging for mercy all the way. Mercy that was not forthcoming. The warrior wears this shame like a badge as he rests on the hill, readying himself to once more combat the creatures that consumed the stars.

Screams snap him back to the present. Those Black Things approach. Ten billion lives dangle by a single, silver thread. Too many innocents depend on his light, too many to repeat his father's failures. He rises once more and waits for the beasts to appear. He stands in a pile of their melting, shadow corpses. Casualties from their last engagement. They shudder away in the night, still jerking in death throes long after he cleaved life from their nebulous forms, leaking into nothingness until all around him hangs a black mist, obscuring his vision.

He does not wait long, they arrive in moments. The voids that rend at flesh and soul, lives defined back their lack thereof. He cannot see them in the dark, but he hears their scraping footsteps. Their snarling mouths, full of misshapen teeth and tongues marred by gangrene, snap hungrily, announcing their ever closer presence.

For a moment, he freezes. His father's fear exists in him still, not entirely purged by his shame. Again he remembers his words as they sat together and watched the emptying sky.

"What makes a great man?" Back then, he never knew how to answer.

Now, he speaks aloud. "Everyone has a choice. Succumb to fear, die begging, pleading on their knees for mercy... or overcome it. You can confront the monsters that growl at us from the shadows, or be consumed by them. There are some things, some people, worth dying for. Once you realize that, once you accept it, there is nothing left but the doing."

Now surrounded by creatures of darkness, he smiles, no longer afraid. He raises his blade aloft—a ray of golden sunshine, razor sharp and hewn from the embers of the last cratering star—and cries the mantra of the bold:

"Opere et Veritate!" *In action and truth!*

So emboldened, he leaps into the fray once more.

The Urn

Mother always wanted to be buried at sea. Laura and I pledged, after she died, that we would make that happen. So from the Kansas flatlands we traveled west by train, on new-laid track through forest and desert and rain.

Weeks passed in silence. We promised we would never speak again of that night, and circumstance had left us with little else. Laura sat by the window. Though she did not say it, I think she loved to watch the landscape rolling by. Watching her, she seemed to age thirty years, the burden of sin. She became the mirror image of the parent we lost. Once, she caught me looking at her and frowned, hard black eyes like coal penetrating to the core of my thoughts.

"I'm not like her, you know. I swear I never will be!"

I nodded in response, silently making the same promise.

As we traveled, Mother waited in the luggage rack in a plain, unadorned urn, returned to dust as we all will be some day. She rolled around above our heads, looming nearly as large in death as she did in life. When the conductor came to take our tickets, he noticed the urn with a start. After that we were left alone. The mysterious children. The couriers of death.

Eventually, our journey ended. We came to California. We wound through the streets, following our noses to the sea. It was vaster than we had ever imagined, stretching out past the limit of our eyesight. We waited for evening, until the sun began to crash beneath the horizon, Mother in hand.

"Bury me." She said, spitting blood. "Bury me where I daren't rise again. Bury me beneath the weight of the ocean. Bury me with the setting sun. Promise me you'll see this through. For the good of the world. Promise me!"

She clutched my hand, which still clenched the knife buried in her side, and convulsed, and screeched. Then fell still. Her emerald eyes faded and were black as I closed them a final time.

I opened the urn, grabbed two nearby rocks, and dumped them into the ash. Resealing the urn, I took my sister's hand, looked her in her cobalt eyes and walked onto a rock outcropping that extended over deep ocean waters. Here, in San Francisco, we consummated a funeral deferred. We had no words, no fond memories of our time with Mother. When we knew her, it was as a woman possessed. The time before, when she was gentle still, remained shrouded in the past. Flashes of kindness. The echo of a smile. The laughter we remember as toddlers. A time as distant to us as Mother was now.

Yet I felt that one of us should speak before the deed was done.

"Earth to Earth," I whispered, "Ashes to Ashes, Dust to Dust."

The urn sank into the ocean depths quickly. Within seconds, all we saw were the waves.

After a moment, Laura finished my thought. "And may dust be all that remains."

We watched the ocean for a while. Watched the tide recede. Watched as the moon rose to replace the sun, bathing the world in faint silver light. Watched to see if the urn would resurface. Clasped together, my hands trembled. I hoped that Laura did not notice. Hours crept by, until satisfied, I turned to leave the burial ground.

Laura waited a while longer, whispering a silent prayer before following. Ahead of her, in the night, I did not then notice her smile.
 I did not notice: her once jet black eyes glowed emerald green.

End And Beginning

Picture the unfathomable darkness of the nowhere the universe has become. A black the pitch of moonless night, but instead of centered in the sky, it is everywhere. The whole of existence collapses in on itself, the crunch of entropy come to bear on a limitless expanse once filled with vibrance, with color. Now all is sublimed in frigid emptiness, and silence. God casts his canvas in shadow. No hint of the paint beneath remains. Nothing breaths, nothing moves, and nothing lives.

Nothing, except for…

One bright light in the corner of the frame. Glowing, burning, it dwindles, recedes, fades, then gathers itself again and fights to expand against the tide of absolute zero. Here lies the everything that once spread over several billion light-years, now smaller than an atom, barely a quark of light left to battle against nightfall. Listen closely, and inside it you hear the ghosts of those the universe once contained. A cacophonous song, a dirge, a chorus in a million different languages. Here is voiced the anguish, the joy, the relief that their struggles have come to an end, the sadness that so too has passed their time with loved ones. So many things left unsaid, so many sentiments impossible to vocalize. And all that remains is light.

Were there any observer to peer into the light, to listen to its song, they might entertain its visions. That of a blue-green world circling around a yellow star. First it sings of its creation, burning dust and effluence cooling and coalescing around an iron-nickel core. It sings of the rain clouds, of the water that patters against the still-soft surface, filling its dimples as oceans. Life sludges forth from its oceans, first mindless protozoa. Eukaryotes with no sense of place swim and crawl of microscopic flagella. Those develop into primitive plant-life, into the first animals that, on some small level, perceive their own existence. Reptilian creatures, increasingly mobile mammals, love and destruction follow. A song that burns as brightly as it ends, with a pockmarked and radioactive surface. Lifeless, yet the planet still turns.

The light also sings of an endless stretch of stars, of nebulae wherein hide creatures the size of galaxies. They swim through space-dust, subsiding on ice and on the stars themselves. They speak to each other in burst of radiation, penetrating the void's gloom on aquiline paths. Brilliant lights cast by celestial beasts. In the collision of these lights, more such creatures are born. Star orcas crafted of molten rock, organic comets obscured by dust clouds light-years thick.

The light sings of life beyond imagining. Invisible minds constructed of song and scent. A network of intelligence that extends through the universe. One heart, several souls, they dream of connection and thus seek the known reality for like beings. But they are alone. As were we all.

Across the quark that possesses all these memories passes an invisible hand, stoking the fire. The only presence that burns still in a universe gone fallow. A voice, from nowhere, from everywhere, from here and from beyond, whispers into the light, reminding it of a once glorious purpose.

What was… will be.

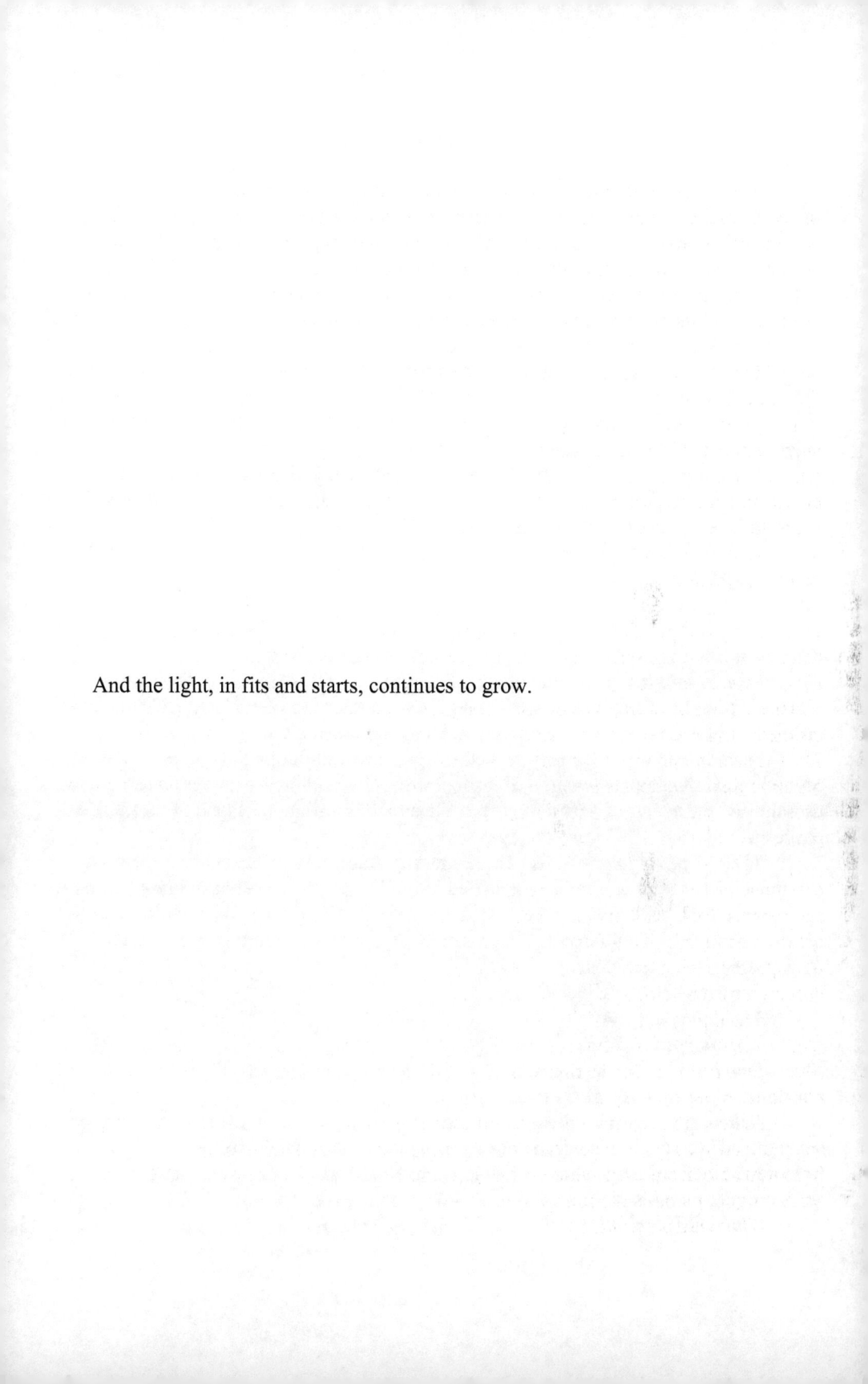

And the light, in fits and starts, continues to grow.

Creation Myths: The Dreamscape

All began with the eternal and ubiquitous Id. A sea of life churning in the void. In that sea Androgiin swam alone. Androgiin, Ego and First Consciousness, the Builder, saw the nothingness that was the Id and the glory that might be. There Androgiin decided: they would give all for the world that is.

Let it begin again. The Builder proclaimed. And so began dancing. Androgiin whirled, a dervish through tenebrous emptiness, its steps a blueprint, its self the stock of creation.

From twinkling eyes that saw and sacrificed swelled the heavens, the sun and blinding stars.

From a body that nurtured and died grew the earth, an expanse of high mountains, deep valleys and endless desert.

From a mouth forever lapsed into silence whispered the wind, followed by a procession of howling storms. From its tears came the rain, filling basins that became the lakes, seas, and the boundless ocean.

From begetting loins, castrated and cast about the cosmos, sprouted flora and sprung fauna of every stripe. Birds to cloud the skies, creatures to leap through forest and field

From a mind that gazed at the deep and wondered, then forgot itself as it dispersed, came awareness, the seed of humankind and of Gods.

From a soul that yearned came the Dreamscape. The demesne of the Id, the Dreamscape floated above, behind, and just beyond the realm Androgiin created, flitting always out of sight, trembling with power. Here lay tamed a limitless potential.

and from its self, the many aspects of One, came children most prized—five faces of the Eternal: Angaama, paragon of justice, wise Wysheid the teacher, Alur, ardent and carnal, Jev, the avatar of destruction, and Eleazar, the smiling fool, one of tricks, of shadows.

With all parts given to this new beginning, Androgiin faded, subliming into all it had made. What little that remained drifted to the corners of existence, no more than bits and pieces of the once glorious Ego. As it diffused, the Gods wept and beat their breasts, terrified babes in the wilderness. They were young, powerful being who could not countenance being left alone.

Father/Mother, Mother/Father!
My children...
Why do you leave us?
Leave you? Look at yourselves, at Creation. Every bit of everything is me. Do not think of me as gone, but transformed.

Naked, still on their knees, damp tears dripping down their cheeks, the Gods were not satisfied. Most wounded of all was Eleazar, the God of Tricks. He who was born his face draped in permanent shadow, a wide smile etched like a scar from cheek to cheek and two large eyes—small black irises swimming in seas of white.

Why make us at all?" He muttered. *"What are we for?*

Androgiin's reply echoed from the world itself, from frosted mountaintops and streams hushing through nascent forests, from the stars above and cyclones rumbling across a newborn Earth, from creatures tottering out on unsure legs and blinking at the bright rays of a neonate sun.

You are stewards. Guide this crafted Ego with passion, wisdom, fervor, righteousness... humor. Protect them from the Id that is their baser nature.

Stay with us! Show us the path. Came their pained reply.

I am. Have been. Will always be of and with you. Remember that my children. Remember...

And with that, The Builder lapsed into silence and was no more. The Newborn Gods were left alone on their freshly molded world. Only Eleazar heard the quiet voice, whispering in his ear as they began to wander a still soft Earth.

Remember, one day the time will come. I will return.

The Scorpion and the Frog

We had fallen together for many centuries before I finally spoke:

"You know what's funny? Well, what I think is funny at least. Most readers believe a story is built of nothing more than the words used to tell it, a common mistake to be sure. They follow their structure, plot and character, ignoring the ur-tale that looms beneath. Take, for example, the common parable of the scorpion and frog. I will recount it to you now; you tell me what the story is about:

"Once, many years ago, a scorpion tired of his mountain home. He began to travel down through the woods, to see what else his world contained. During his journey, he came to a stream he wished to cross. There, on the bank, played a frog. The scorpion approached the amphibian and asked to frog to carry him on his back to the other side.

"'How do I know you won't sting me?' The frog asked, naturally wary of the arachnid's venomous tail.

"The scorpion replied: 'Because if I do, I'll die too. I'll drown.'

"The frog, satisfied, allowed the scorpion to hop on, and began to travel through the current. It was the beginning of spring, and the melting snow had swelled the river's current to a torrent that almost dragged them both under. But the frog fought on, swam through it. A noble creature he held up his end of the bargain and made it through the worst of the flow.

"However, as they approached the other side, he felt a painful sting. Looking around, he saw that the scorpion had indeed stuck him. Paralysis rapidly setting in, he gurgled. 'Scorpion, why did you kill me? Now you have doomed us both.'

"The scorpion shrugged, or approximated a shrug as best as scorpions know how. 'I couldn't help it. You see, it's just my nature…'

"So, entangled together, they sank beneath the waves.

"Now, tell me, what is that story about? The impossibility of creatures to overcome their baser natures? How it is God's will that beasts do what they were created to do—the frog to swim, the scorpion to sting? Both to die? Or is it something else?"

I smile, tail swishing in the dark.

"Once, many years ago, I tired of my home. The sulfur, the burning heat, the emptiness. I climbed out of the void to see what else the universe contained. I came across many wonders, dying stars, thick clouds of nebulae, worlds with nascent intelligent life slouching towards self-destruction. Looming over creation, I collected it all within me.

"Eventually I came to a barrier I could not pass, the end of this known demesne. A blank wall, a ferocious current of nothingness. And there you were, my nemesis, waiting to see what came next.

"'Why should I carry you across?' You asked when I approached. 'He who was banished, carried by I who banished you? Surely you jest. Will you not touch your anti-matter to my matter, thus cancelling out both our powers?'

"'But then we would both sink into nothing. I would also drown in the void between universes.'

"You nodded at the sense of that, and so we entered and, well, you know what came next. My sting. Here we are still falling. Even those creatures within me, ignorant of oblivion, tell this tale in their own way as we hurtle down through the black. On a molecular or spiritual level, they know what I have done, what this story is about: the consumption of their known universe. How it all will end, has ended, with we two creatures of the cosmos tumbling off the edge into nowhere.

"What? No smile, no comment, no condemnation? Not even a rebuke. You've said nothing since we entered this null-space. How many times can I apologize? How often must I explain?

"You see... it's just my nature."

It Gets Better

The Hereafter wasn't quite what Antoine expected. No fire, no army of demons. Merely an ambling desert, uncertain footing atop shifting sands for as far as the eye could see. There was no sun, but heat bore down on him regardless. His feet burned black on sand hotter than a furnace fire. The young, yet damned soul trudged beneath an empty sky, bereft of any color. Not blue, not red, no matte arrangement of stars, just emptiness, as if the land he tread was all that mattered. This must be Hell, Antoine knew, there was nowhere else it could be. This perdition was not nearly as horrible as he expected.

And yet... yet...

How he longed to have someone else to talk to. Alone on the plain, no wind, no noise except for the smacking of chapped, bleeding lips—he thirsted, he hungered, but did not die. He felt himself slipping into madness. Isolation, the most effective torture Satan could develop for mankind's social soul. Antoine would have tipped his hat to the fallen angel, were he wearing one. This was a subtle Hell indeed.

How he craved a drink. His throat coated with sand. Every swallow brought more abrasions along his esophagus. Antoine bled internally from a thousand tiny cuts. Each breath flushed his insides with desert air, drying him out a little more. He took a step, and then another, less sure with each one why he bothered moving at all. Perhaps it was time to lie down, maybe he needed sleep. Just for a while... or for good. What difference did it make, after all, to the dead?

"It gets better."

Antoine blinked in shock. Time passed him by with indifference, and he did not know how many forevers had come and gone since last he heard another voice. Here one was hanging in the air. The young man looked around trying to find its source, hands shaking with... fear? Yes, and excitement and hope. Something had changed in a static world.

"Hello?" He asked, and his own voice shocked him, a loud baritone that cut through the quiet and quickly disappeared among absorbent dunes. "Who's there?"

"Well, first it gets worse... but it does eventually get better." The voice again came from all around Antoine. He could not place it. The air itself comforted him, or so it seemed. Was this a trick? Another means to propel him down the path of madness? He tried to weep, but no more moisture availed itself. He was a husk dragging through nowhere to get to nowhere, forgotten by all but Death's faceless jester who taunted him from the abyss.

"You aren't mad. Hopelessness is normal, given these circumstances. We're about as far down as a man can fall." The man spoke again, for it was a man's voice, and this time it did have a direction. Antoine lifted his head and in the distance he saw a speck, a moving shadow, another life in the wilderness. He did not wonder then how it was he heard this man speaking like he was already in his midst, running gladly to him like the stranger brought with him an oasis of the coolest water. Sooner than he thought possible, they met, touching calloused fingertip to calloused fingertip.

Wheezing with exertion, the young soul spoke first. "An-Antoine."

"I'm sorry?"

"My-my... oh God, my name. It's Antoine. Who are you? Where did you come from? W-why why are you-" Antoine stopped to catch his breath.

"-am I here?" The other man smiled, just another crease on a face well-traveled with lines and folds, greyed with impossible age. He scratched his scalp, cracked and bare. "I suppose that will be apparent soon enough. All in Lou's time."

"Lou?"

"My pet name for our jailer. You know, Lucifer?" The old stranger smiled through every word, unnerving Antoine.

"Where I'm from..." The man continued, taking the questions in reverse order. "A place, much like this, empty. A void suited best for limitless pain. My time there was done, so I was brought here. Now, as for my name-" He paused a while, chapped, pale lips pursed in thought. "You know, I don't remember. It's been so long since it was any use."

Antoine shifted uneasily from burnt foot to burnt foot. Suddenly, with a visitor to his hollow realm, he was conscious of his near nakedness in the thin rags that draped his emaciated body. He was a skeleton coat hanger for fabric bleached colorless by the heat. That the other man dressed similarly brought little comfort.

"So, uh," Antoine spoke, uncertain how to proceed, "Uh... what happens now?"

"Suppose, in lieu of my name, I tell you a story. You'll learn more about me that way than any name'd teach."

The young, dead man nodded in assent.

"When I was, oh, just about your age I'd guess, I killed a man. I can't now remember why. Maybe it was over something foolish like lust or love, but reasons matter less than consequences. The man died all the same, by my hands, in my arms." As he spoke, the old soul traced a pattern in the sand with his toe—a spiral growing slowly outward.

"I didn't confess. The crime was never solved. I remember... pretending to cry at his funeral, being comforted by gathered friends and family. I suppose I must have known him rather well. Anyway, years passed. I married, had children, lived what many might consider a 'good life', and died at a ripe old age. And yet still, despite all that good papered over the sin I-"

"You ended up here." Antoine interrupted in spite of himself, quietly cursing his rudeness.

The old man smiled, not appearing to mind the disruption. What was a little time lost to the dead?

"That's right, I ended up here. For the longest time I was alone in a desert, like you. Unlike yours, mine was a tundra. So cold I could feel my blood freezing in my veins. With every breath I swallowed hundreds of sharp icicles. Each moment birthed unendurable pain. I shuffled along for God knows, well... maybe not, how long. Days, months, millennia. Until I heard a voice."

"'It gets better.'" Antoine intoned, unconsciously mimicking the old man's voice.

"At first it was impossible to tell where it came from. But then I saw her, in the distance, no more than a mite on the horizon. Faster than I thought possible, there I was in her arms. She told me her story. Her sin is not important, but it was vile. A rough in a vale of diamonds. I asked her the same question you asked me: Why are you here?

"'To make you see.'"

See what? Antoine wanted to ask, but he waited. The answers came in due course.

"And that's also why I am here, Antoine. To make you see."

Then Antoine did ask. "See what?"

The old man shook his head, instead asking. "Tell me about your life."

And so Antoine did, or so he thought. He spoke of his childhood, a hard drinking mother and father both passing in an out of prison, never really a presence in his life. The aunts and uncles whose hands he passed through, whose hands often found themselves on him in places they shouldn't. The grandfather who taught him how to shoot a gun, then placed him on a street corner at the young age of 12, pockets full of 'dust'. He spoke of the life he took a year later, and how he regretted the violence each time. He spoke of his dreams, the poetry he wrote in secret and told only to the boys and girls who frequented his bed. He spoke of his too young death, and stopped, looking at the old man expectantly.

The old soul frowned and again shook his head. "No, tell me the truth."

Again Antoine recounted his life, not sure what the old man wanted. This time he discussed more detail about the darkness that brought him here. How his hands shook after each kill, though less and less each time. About getting high in back alleys, selling to kids even younger than himself. He confessed to killing his grandfather, then his parents, once he realized he could sustain himself without their interference. He admitted that sometimes, after reading his lovers his secret poetry, his knife would dance across their flesh so that they could tell no one else, and how he'd find someone new to play with. Tears in his eyes each time. He told of his death, shot in the back by someone he never saw. He remembered fading as their hands went through his pockets, and then the dull pain as they stabbed his dying flesh, once, twice, three times for good measure. And then he was here. Again he finished and looked back up at the old man.

He pursed his lips and sighed. "I said the truth, boy."

This time, Antoine recounted his tale without emotion. There was no justification. No weeping. No humanizing his actions. Just a list of sins, a long and varied catalogue of transgressions. There was so much wrong. So much hurt wrought by his hands and his alone. Confronting it again and again, the young man rubbed off the scabs over his guilt and finally saw all the pain he caused others. He saw this pain was all that mattered. No one saw how you suffered inside. No one cared about the motivations for your evil. All people see is what you do. The 'why' of anything is pointless before the weight of the 'what'.

The old man finally nodded. And the young soul found that, despite how low he felt delving into his past again and again, the telling lightened him somewhat. He fell to the ground and might have died of gratitude then and there were his heart still beating. It was over. He could hurt no one else now, not even himself.

"Like I told you, it gets worse at first, but then…" The voice echoed from all around him again and when the young soul looked up, he was not surprised to find the old man gone. Nor was he worried that he no longer remembered his own name. His sins, all he truly was, stood tall in his memory.

"It gets better," He finished the sentence that hung in the hot desert, then sat down to wait, no longer burned by the sand.

See No Evil, Hear No Evil

Oslo watched the second-hand race around the clock, counting down to midnight on the eve of his 25th birthday, and imagined he could still hear it ticking. In a way, he could. As sound-waves crashed against his cochlear sea, he felt the vibration, but that was all it was. Feeling. Sensation, but no noise. His head hummed in silence. Fingers pressed flat against the table, he knew it rained outside by the patter that rattled along his palms. He sniffed, and smelled Rosco, their black Labrador, scratching around in the backyard. Ammonia, judging by the pungent scent, it would not be long until he found his way back to their door, scratching and—presumably—whining to be let back in. The young man picked up a pen in brown hands and wrote a few final lines, completing a story inspired by his year in meditation.

They say that deafness is like sleep, and sound like a world we can never wake into. That a Writer's world digs ever inward. We plumb the soul while Talkers ascend to the heavens. But here, inside my head, I found a heaven that is all my own. My only fear is that—if I remain trapped here long enough—I will find it a hell before too long.

It was then the young man, trapped by indecision, had the choice made for him by time. Sound rushed around him, over him, through him, from the far off cries of babes to the beating wings of a nearby insect. He looked down at the words he had just written, and it did not matter when later they became smudged illegible with tears: after all, no matter how clear they were, he would never again read them.

He became what we all fear most: a Writer damned to Listen.

Could I live like this? Forever? He asked himself, replacing the pen on the desk. He had wondered this again and again over the past year, after growing accustomed to interacting with the world by sight and smell and touch, reading along to his favorite movies, nose deep in book after book, looking friends in the face as those who had chosen to speak spoke, and reading the words of the ones who had not in their hands. Oslo closed his eyes, bright grey pools troubled by storms of doubt, and leaned back in his chair. Interlocking his fingers in his frizzy hair, now buzzed close to his head, he felt he could distinguish each individual stubble. If he concentrated he might even feel it growing, however slowly, from his scalp. Heightened senses were the gift to every man and woman who came of majority age. He opened his eyes. They found the clock again, inexorably ticking towards the moment of decision. 60, 59, 58 seconds away. Soon, there would be no turning back.

He was reflecting on this same moment a year prior, when he finished testing life as a Talker, relishing the richness of laughter—how full the world felt when you could hear and yet how empty your head, looking at row after row of books, knowing their contents, their worlds, were never to be yours—when his Mother ascended the steps to his room in the attic. She waited a moment on the stairs, not wanting to interrupt his reverie, his collection of sensory data. She remembered from her own youth how important it was to consider every experience and every sensation, in order to best decide which one you could do without.

Then the clock struck 12, each bell a silent tremor. At their end, like a drowning man pulled from the sea, noise came crying back to Oslo's ears. He heard the rain, heard Roscoe barking, the laughter and chatter of the assembled party guests awaiting his decision. Tonight was his Sense Fete. Where his manhood would be celebrated and his loss mourned; where he would be carried across the threshold into the world where some spoke and listened but could not read, and others wrote and studied but did not hear. His mother finished climbing the stairs as the final bell rang and Oslo turned 25. Her eyes were dry, but red, and, with the Writer's waning keen sense, Oslo smelled that the handkerchief in her back pocket was damp with tears.

"Well my son, have you made a decision?" Her voice trembled as she feared what she was about to lose. Would her beloved son never speak to her again, and be destined to a life of the mind? Would he become a recluse who gradually recedes from the only world she understood? Would he sacrifice the books he loved? The academic pursuits that sustained him? Would he choose to remain drowning in sound, in humanity's flow?

The young man did not answer right away, racing through his memories of this year and the one prior. When had he felt the most joy? Was it hearing his friend tell a favorite joke? Or those long nights spent in a basement library? Was it in movies? Or the moments of meditation where the world seemed bright and the truth clear? Was it surrounded by friends and loved ones? Or isolation?

He closed his eyes and remembered...

He brushed Oslo's hand, catching his attention, and smiled. His eyes were bright, those of one who had consumed a hundred worlds and then a hundred more. Who had heard everything worth saying and found it wanting. Who had wisdom to offer in text... and in touch? In sight and in smell. Who communicated in that moment, with that gesture and that grin and those beckoning eyes, more than he remembered any man could with a hundred thousand spoken words at his disposal.

Oslo followed the young man into the backroom, where nothing needed to be said.

Oslo opened his eyes and smiled—a poor imitation of that boy's own, he whose name he had never learned nor needed to—and took his pen in hand. His Mother's gentle sobs began to fade, the last sounds he would ever hear. He treasured them.

Yes, I have.

The Reflection

There are places, there are hidden spaces, the frigid peak of a mountain or a basement corner in a condemned mansion, where the world wears thin. One can stand there and peer into another universe. One that exists just behind, just above, just outside our own. In one such place a young man stood and waited for his reflection. The other mind behind the mirror. He who stopped mimicking his movements one day and winked, realizing the lost dream of Narcissus.

He knew what they planned to do in those woods was dangerous. As luck would have it, the forest behind his house—a land of strange sightings and unsolved disappearances, was one such space where worlds collided. He knew they hazarded the whole of not just his world, or his reflection's, but the total of creation itself. But from that first moment when he realized that hidden in that glass was another life, with a smile so like his own, he knew they had no choice. They had to meet, to touch, and to know each other's intimate spaces.

After a few minutes of waiting, he saw a transparent copy of himself approach through the forest. The same full lips, the same dark curly hair cropped close to the scalp, the same dark skin, ashy and cracking against the winter cold. The reflection smiled, and he knew it to be identical to his own. How many times had he seen the same crooked smile in the mirror? Dimpled and gap-toothed. He memorized it, and to see it replicated so perfectly by another thrilled him

They stood, face to face, under the auspices of an ancient oak. The wind blew and snow that fell the night before swirled down among them from the boughs, matting his hair, falling through his reflection like he was not wholly there. They did not speak right away, letting the mist from their breath come together and then dissipate like they might do soon, like the universe might.
He was unsure what to say and so, he sensed, was his twin.

"You came." He finally stammered.
"I did, so did you. I didn't think-"
"No, neither did I."

It was, as he suspected, like talking to himself. The same voice and speech patterns. Yet, somehow he sensed, there was another soul here. Another life apart from his own with its own memories and experiences. His reflection looked up at the sky, gray and austere. The omnipresent cloud cover of a New England winter.

"Well that's one difference. In my world, it's summer."

He looked behind his reflection, and saw—though faint—the same land and trees, but instead of leafless and bows laden with snow, the trees were blooming and covered in leaves. The sky was clear, the sun was just beginning to rise. They stood in grass, but somehow also in snow. He was cold and warm at the same time, and his feet were damp, the ice melting into water as it became unsure which world it belonged to.

"Should we do this?"
"Do what?"
"This, meet like this. Touch… you hear stories."

"Yeah, present and past selves meet. The timeline collapses on itself. That kind of thing? Not really the same situation here."

He kicked the snow, now slush, not wanting to look his reflection in the eyes.

"No, but it could be like... so the universe is made of matter and anti-matter. When the two meet, an incredible amount of energy is released. A cataclysmic amount even. Is it right to risk our... worlds? Our everything? Over this?"

His reflection frowned, thinking for a while how best to answer.

"Let me ask you something. When we first met, and realized that we were more than just an image. When you discovered I was your light, and you mine, how did you feel?"

He closed his eyes and remembered. His incredulity at the impossibility of it. The joy at discovering a like mind.

"The sun rose after years of night. I grew legs and crawled up out of the ocean and onto the shore. I was blind and trapped in a box, but you let me out and taught my eyes to see. I felt... like..." Words failed him.

His reflection nodded.

"I felt the same. You ask, is it worth risking the universe to consummate... whatever this is. I ask, what else is the universe for if not this precise moment? What else is there but us?"

"A bit solipsistic, no?"

The reflection took another step closer. Their noses were almost touching. He felt his reflection's breath on his cheek. As they talked, he grew more solid, as did the world behind him along with its sun. He could see his reflection shivering and knew his winter encroached as well.

"Perhaps, but look around you. In both worlds, at this moment, there is no one but us. Let's be a little selfish, let's..." And instead of finishing his thought, he closed his eyes and leaned forward.

He means to kiss me. The man realized. Then he smiled. *Well, why not?*

He leaned forward as well, and their lips touched. And, in that perfect moment, it mattered little to either of them whether their universes ended or not.

He opened his eyes to darkness, felt his reflection's arms around him. He was an idea no longer, but love made flesh. His feet touched nothingness and yet he stood. He was not cold, not hot, not afraid despite that absolute emptiness around them. There was no light, yet he saw the man across from him perfectly. He saw himself, skin only slightly lighter than the absolute night. He was smiling, and he knew that smile reflected his own. The young man smiled back, took his reflection's hand, and they leaned forward to kiss again.

There was no light, no sound, no world, no wind. Only love remained.

The Night Has A Thousand Eyes
The night has a thousand eyes,
And the day but one;
Yet the light of the bright world dies
With the dying of the sun.

    Looking back, the Mothers would say they recognized her destiny straight away, and were glad the next savior would be one of their own. A rose-colored half-lie to obscure a darker truth. They knew, indeed, but hoped against hope they were wrong. They wanted to spare their daughter the pain forced upon all Messiah's, the burden of guiding the flock through an unforgiving wilderness.

    Maraya did not cry, not once. Not when exiting the womb. Not when they cut the cord. Not when blinking as she adjusted to the light in the 'sky' that mimicked the sun. She watched with quiet gray eyes as the conclave swaddled her, as if when first coming into this world, she remembered their births. As if when she closed her eyes to sleep that night, she could see the blue and the clouds of the world that was. Maraya smiled in her sleep, like she felt the long-forgotten stars kiss her plump cheeks in the night.

    She was a precocious child. For the first year she watched and listened. Every moment she was learning, and on the eve of her first birthday she spoke, broken and malformed English trickled out her soft palette.

    "Ee ha'e so fa t'o."

    At first, the Mothers took it as little more than the pidgin gurglings of a young girl. Sounds with no more meaning than the emotion behind them.

    "You hungry, baby child?" One cooed, her Birther, baring herself for feeding.

    Maraya shook her head. This struggle, to make herself understood. She swam upwards from the bottom of the sea of infancy, flexing the long arms of language that she had grown, but never before used.

    "We… ha-ave… so far… t'go."

    The Birther, Belledonne, stopped with her arms by her side. Language? In a child so young? She exchanged a glance with the others. All knowing what such precocity forecast for her future. The Captain had to know. With a nod, the Farmer—Ertrude—left the nursery and quickly wound her way through the reeds towards the steps winding into the sky.

    And so, as the lights dimmed to mimic twilight, she came. A lithe figure in gray-suit, the mothers were always surprised by how small she was in truth. Compared to the power of her spirit, how her authority loomed. To see her was to remember that she herself was no bigger than a child, though there was no denying the ancient wisdom in her eyes. Dark and black like space itself, they betrayed nothing, but remembered everything.

    She pursed her lips, clenching and unclenching her hands as she approached the babe at the center of the room. She knelt before the bassinet, feeling the gray eyes watching her as she brought her face to the child's height. They watched each other a while before the Captain spoke.

"We have so far to go."

The child spoke slowly, deliberately, recalling a ritual she only half-understood, wanting for every word to be clear.

"Our... world is... only... a memory."

"Only the Captains remember."

"Only... they... shall... see... us... home."

"We are..."

"Ee, We... are..."

"The Captains." They finished in unison, not once blinking as they held the other's gaze. The Captain, white hair curled up around her had in a shock of an afro, nodded, her lips a thin line of grim satisfaction. Here lay not a child, but an equal.

She turned to the Mothers, who gave the two a wide berth as they commiserated.

"She is the one. When she's old enough. Send her to me."

Belledonne was frightened, but not too frightened to ask what needed asking.

"And when, O Mother, will we know the time is right?"

The Captain did not turn back, only paused briefly at the burlap flap that hid the nursery from the glare of a false star.

"You'll know." And she was gone, weaving back through the tall grass.

The Mothers stood in silence a while. Then crowded back around the crib of their beloved Maraya. She whose name would be stripped away. Whose very identity would be subsumed in time.

"I'm sorry, my darling." They crowed in unison. "I'm sorry! Roan has claimed you. There is nothing left but to go."

The child did not speak, talking correctly to the Captain had drained her. All that remained was the energy to be the baby she was. But her thoughts were clear in her gaze.

This was always my fate. There is no use regretting the things that are certain.

Regardless, tears streaked her cheeks. She closed her eyes and remembered the night sky. The true night sky. The darkness with its countless distant lights that they streaked past and towards in the Arc, their vessel, its payload humankind's only hope. The stars weighed upon her like a hundred thousand piercing eyes. Each perhaps with a world or two of their own. One perhaps with a world meant for her flock... but perhaps not. Perhaps they would die in space, lost and cold and forgotten. Perhaps she would fail.

And for the first time in her short life, on the morning of her first birthday, Maraya, the next Captain, wailed.

> *The mind has a thousand eyes,*
> *And the heart but one;*
> *Yet the light of a whole life dies*
> *When love is done.*
> *--Francis William Bourdillon*

The Earthbound Shade

After a long, Earthly slumber, your spirit takes Father Time's hand. He leads you to the stars, introduces you to the man you could have been. At first, you do not understand. Flying past distant pinpoints of light you look through your translucent hands and wonder: "Am I… really?"

The Elder Father Time responds with a quick nod. Faint hands gripped in his opaque, brown mitts, your shade appears even more insubstantial.

"Yes. Your time is done. The course of your life carved in stone."

His voice is deep like the space around you, vast like many universes. Its inexorable timbre pulls your soul past the event horizon. No use in denying the obvious. No point fighting life's end. For a while, neither of you speak as Father Time guides you upwards into the black. You, the shade, parse what it means to become meaningless.

It is too big to be seen, the unreality of nonexistence. It is too much to confront all at once. And yet you must, to see what comes next.

Eventually, they slow, hovering over a familiar sight. The shade beholds a blue-green orb, large swaths of its surface obscured by white.

"But this is-"

"Yes… and no."

"How is that possible?

"The world you knew was one of many possible worlds that are, or might or will be."

Father Time continues: "We travel not just through what, but through when. Back in time to a different Earth, where you are a different you.

"I take you to see the differences between your many souls, your countless hearts. What changes... and what does not. I take you to see the core of your being. Only once you understand that, will you understand what must happen next."

You shake your see-through head, hoping futilely to clear away cobwebs of confusion, omnipresent since the onset of death. "I don't unders-"

"No? You will. Watch." Suddenly you descend, down into the clouds towards a familiar landmass. Down into a familiar city and quiet home.

It is you, the shade, but alive. Much is the same, yet much is also different. This self wears different clothes, speaks a different tongue. Yet, connected by a kinship of the soul, you understand. And as you understand you remember. You knows what horror you are about to witness.

Your ghost turns to Father Time, near tears. "Please, please, don't make me watch-"

"You must."

"Please, I understand. I get it. Let me go… send me to hell. Whatever my fate is supposed to be. Just don't make me-"

"Watch."

You, the shade, try to close your eyes, but still can see the scene through translucent lids. You turn away, but the world turns with you. Father Time regards you without sympathy, his dark brow creases.

"You will watch. There is no escaping what you do, what you will do, what you have done."

And so, despite your eyes shut tight, you do. You watch yourself, a different self, slowly sip a glass of wine. Your smile open and hungry. You watch the man, your mirror image, fingers lingering over a tray of knives, grin at the figure bound to a chair at his dining room table.

"Where shall we begin?" He/You ask over muted screams, tutting mockingly at the struggling victim. "Now, now, we discussed this."

You/He selects an enormous cleaver with a thin, sharp blade. Handle shimmering in the firelight, its inlay bejeweled with glowing emeralds. You/He caress your victim to be with the blade, a thin wound tracing your path.

"No one can hear you. Not in this house, high on this hill. No one is coming to save you."

And so, madness flirting with his gaze, your doppelgänger dances around the room. Long, slow and with many steps, yours is a terrible art. For a while, you cannot tell if the screams are your victim's or your own. However, after much torture, then dismemberment, there is no longer any doubt. Only you are left to scream Father Time forces you to watch the whole grisly deed, to see what glee you took in the bloody work. See what pools at and through your feet.

You turn to the wizened Father and again beseech.

"Please, I get it. I do. I… just, take me away. Anywhere but here. Anywhere. Anywhere…"

The old, dark man looks to you, his mouth a thin, sad line. He again does not speak, but his face says enough: Be careful what you wish for. He lifts you both back up into the heavens, back to the void and stars. Again you travel through space and time, alighting on another Earth.

Immediately, you know what you will see. "No, please, not again. I meant-"

"What you meant is immaterial. This is your fate. It is your own doing."

Here, on this Earth, you follow a young man in a dim alley. From the smile on his face, he clearly expects a different sort of encounter.

"So," He laughs, "What did you want to-" He stops laughing immediately upon seeing your gun.

"Wait, wait. I'll do anything. Just please d-"

Your only reply is gunfire. Its retort loud even in the rainy night. People flock to the alley, but we are already gone. On to the next Earth. And on and on. The methods and means change, but the result is always the same. You are always the same monster, with an unslakable thirst. At first you beg, plead with Father Time to show no more. You throw myself at the hem of his celestial garment, shimmering with the light of a hundred stars, but to no avail.

Always the refrain: "You must understand."

"But I do! Please make it stop!"

Father Time looks at you, the shade, inscrutable. "No, you don't."

Finally, floating above a world where you dissect your victims. A doctor obsessed with experimentation. You at last ask the right question:

"What will it take for me to understand? How do I make this stop?"

At first, it looks like Father Time will not answer, a tortured silence. But after a pause, he sighs, with empathy in his glimmering eyes that are bright like the stars and just as distant. He relents, just this once.

"You still don't understand. There are countless universes. Within most universes Earth never forms, yet still there are countless Earths... On most Earths, life never comes to be. They are fields, forever fallow. Yet on countless others form vernal pools...

"Even when there is life, the vast section of worlds never birth men, and yet there are limitless iterations of humanity..."

Each word he speaks slowly, each word penetrates a little deeper. "In most human civilizations, you are never born, and yet..."

You finish the thought at its only logical destination. "I am endless. This will never be done... This is... Hell?"

"Someone once wrote 'Hell is other people'," Father Time smirks, "But I prefer to say: Hell is seeing yourself for who you really are."

You do not respond. There is nothing to say. No futile protest to lodge. In the quiet, Father Time senses your understanding. The two of you, jailed and jailor, take flight once more. The two of you disappear into the past, into your many crimes and their frightful symmetry.

As the stars pass you by, and the planets too, you wonder. How many others slip through the void, made to witness sins they would sooner forget?

How many others arrive at this moment? Where they accept Death is a pain that will never end?

When the Wind Speaks...

When the wind speaks, you listen.

So it was, when, one inauspicious morning, a gust of wind whistled through an open window, tousling the hair of the sleeping figure within. The young man woke to a quiet whisper calling *to the beach, to the beach* as he slept alone. He rose quickly and dressed, following the command without hesitation.
One does not question the wind.

It was still cool as the sun rose, the grass beneath his bare-feet damp with dew. He padded silently along the path that led from his modest hut to the shore's black sands. Wandering along, the young man was not sure what he sought—until there it lie—on the edge of the tide. A creature unlike any he had ever seen.

Drawing closer, the young man saw it a human's shape, but its color...

Here—in the One World—lived men of all shapes and all shades. From those dark as rocks born in the belly of dying volcanos, to those the burnt red of the bark on God's proudest trees, to those tone of a ripe, juicy peach, but never, the young man thought as he approached the—sleeping? dead?—figure, had he seen a man so pale. In the growing sunlight he appeared almost translucent. What little of the stranger's skin that was visible outside his bulky, foreign dress seemed pale, unhealthy, like the ash that gathered in the pit of an untended fire. What little hair remained to him ringed his white, dome-like skull—like a shock of old yarn, fraying and molted. The stranger began to stir, eyelids fluttering as he blinked to wakefulness. He started at seeing the young man hovering over him, so the One Worlder crouched close and asked his pressing question:

"Are you... human?"

The strange, ashen-faced man furrowed his brow, before unleashing a bile of strange speech onto the young man's ears. It was a harsh language, unpleasant to the ear and soul, but the young man forced himself to concentrate, to breath in the words. He mumbled a silent prayer for comprehension, and slowly, surely, he began to understand.

"-dashed upon the bloody rocks over there, I suppose the survivors will be along to deal with you savages. We didn't expect anyone to be here in our new home. And you can't even speak civilized tongue? It will be short work deali-"

The young man sighed, and interrupted the man in his own tongue with the same question.

"Are you human?"

At that, the pale-face grew even paler, if possible. "You... you understand? You speak the Queen's tongue? You? A savage? How is that possible?"

The young man replied with the saying his teacher repeated often as he learned the tricks of the wind. "Words are nothing but air, breathe deeply and their meanings reveal themselves."

Regaining composure, the stranger who still lay on the shore brushed the dark sand from his cumbersome coat. "Well—whatever that means, you may serve some use yet." He lifted a hand to the young man without meeting his eyes. "Be a good boy and help me up?"

The young man stared at the hand unmoving, until the stranger rolled his eyes, apparently remembering the unanswered question. "Tch, of course I'm human. I'm more Man that your godless kind. Help me up!"

Muttering another silent prayer, words representing a call to truth that only the wind would know, the young man took the stranger's hand and as they touched, the answer to his benediction came—a premonition of this stranger's dark intentions. An army of ships coming to the One World's shores, on each ship a legion of ashy warriors bearing strange weapons and crying their guttural words of death. Their words promised an end to the One World's way of life, a silencing of the wind. A whispered warning... *all they bring are lies; their only truth death*.

The young man moved, again without hesitating, with the same hand he used to help the stranger up, he pulled him forward, knocking him off balance.

"What are you do-" He interrupted the pale stranger with the dagger drawn with his other hand from the leather sheath at his hip, a quick swipe across the throat. From the red line gushed the dark crimson lifewater that filled every man.

"So, you are human," He spoke the unclean pale-man's language, though its words felt like pebbles choking his throat. Every human-being, despite their provenance, deserved to understand the words following them into death. "The wind says you are human, but that our death comes with you."

The young man crouched again, as the stranger lay now on his back, eyes clouding, mouth wordlessly gaping—a fish flopping its last minutes upon a land it will never understand.

"It is as my teacher always said: 'Death can beget only death'. My apologies for the violence, but it was a preventative measure. Don't worry, I am here to watch you go. You are not alone."

The stranger's empty eyes stared up at the rising sun. His soul returned to whatever strange home had birthed him across the vast sea. Paying his final respect, the young man closed the stranger's eyes. Whatever else he might have been; whatever threat he promised, there was no denying his humanity. As he did so, a gust of wind tumbled along the beach, bringing with it another vision. A shipwreck a little further along the beach, just around the head of a not-too-distant spit. The surviving ashy-ones dragged themselves from the maw of the sunken boat, dragging with them several chests. The wind showed him the contents of a few of that chests, strange weapons that looked like tubes with a small appendage at their base. He saw the men begin to pack them with black metal balls and a fine, dark powder.

Death... this is the death. The wind whispered, and showed the young man the future that might be. The pale men drying these weapons with fire and the heat of the sun, then using those same weapons to raid his village and others like it, spitting that same fire into the face of men, women and innocent children. Burning the corpses of the young man and everyone he loved along the shore before carrying their death inward into the One World.

They must be stopped. Only you can stop them.

The young man, returned to the present from the unpleasant future, blinked the tears from his eyes. Gripping the hilt of his blade so tightly his palm turned the same pale sheen as the dead man at his feet, he began to jog down the beach. Faster and faster he ran until it was a full-blown sprint. As he ran, he offered a breathless plea to the wind.
   "Call my mate," He begged, "Warn my brothers and sisters. Bring them to my aid. Let them know what awaits should I fall. Let them know what has happened here. For… for…" His lungs had no space to finish his prayer as he rounded the beach's sandy head, and saw the wood skeleton ominous in the distance.
   For when the wind speaks…

Ashes to Ashes

He sat in the saloon, on a dusty stool in a dingy room, holding a cold drink in gloved hands. Watching the world burn from hooded eyes. Earth slid after him into darkness. Every eye is upon him. The man of legends. King of Ashes. He who cannot be touched. Each man dreams of the bounty on his head. Each man fears death.

He dumps the brew down his throat, careful to ensure that no part of the glass touches his skin. Swallowing it all in one practiced gulp. A towering presence blocks his light. Its shadow belongs to a large mountain of a man who approaches where no others would dare.

"Are you the man myths claim you are?"

Emptying another glass, he squints up at the bulk: "I am he."

The mountain sits beside him and for a while they drink together and do not speak.

"E'er been down by old Atlante? Once was an outpost there..."

The man sighs. He knows where this is headed. He signals the barkeep for another drink, the prospect of death and the dealing of death was not one he relished sober. Another one of his many sins caught up to him. Another conflict comes, one with only the single possible conclusion.

"And what if I was?"

The mountain turns to face him, eyes simmering in rage.

"How'd you leave it, the town?"

Waiting for his drink, the King of Ashes winces and forces the difficult words out into the open, sealing both their fates.

"As I recall, weren't much left."

He removes the glove from one hand, rests the other on the bar. The man, the tired, aggrieved man stares at the mountain a while as its face contorts with anger and grief. He watches, and imperceptibly, his stance softens. After a while of foisting off the desperate and the vengeful, one can begin to tell the difference between the two. Here sits a desperate man.

Finally, he whispers: "Who did I take from you?"

The mountain starts to weep. "M-my daughter] ."

He stands and approaches the sobbing mountain, resting the still gloved hand on his shoulder. A futile gesture of comfort. He knows what else he offers is of greater worth to this lost cause.

"And... would you like to join her?"

Sniffling, eyes leaking, the large man doesn't answer. But he doesn't reject the King either.

He removes the other glove. Both bare hands, weapons of mass destruction, at the ready.

"I can see it. Beyond the gate she sits and waits... for you. I can bring you there. To the end of your suffering. Where you daughter lingers."

Where he also waits for me...

He shows the mountain his hands. His slight, yet most dangerous, hands.

"I can take you to her. I will, if you wish it."

The mountain thinks, then asks in a mousy tone belying his bulk: "Does it hurt?"

The now gloveless man shakes his head. "Not for long."

The mountain bows his head, answer enough. The King of Ashes touches skin to his skin.

"Sorry" He says, realizing that he too is crying, "I'm sorry."

It happens quickly. Transformation, disintegration, begins in an instant. The mountain's skin grays, grows flaky. His face convulses once, then crumbles away. Where once there flesh, now lies only ash.

The bar's patrons watch as the King dons his gloves, quaffs his beer and exits, never to return. None rise to pursue, despite the lion's bounty on his head. As he leaves, it is not the mountain he sees—his most recent victim—but another, younger face. One that mirrors his own. A face, become gray, that cracks and tumbles away with the wind. His quiet tears become loud sobs. Grief settles upon him yet again.

"My son! My son!"

He mourns in the desert, a speck in the distance wandering away from one more lost watering hole. As always, he is alone.

The Historians

The Historian writes in his book with a blood-red pen, etching events that never happened into existence, erasing many bloody misdeeds from the memory of his world. He stretches to shake away the pain of old age, the weight of many years witnessing the worst, helpless to prevent it, his only duty to change how those who suffered remember.

"It's cleaner this way," He explains, before dreaming of horrors only he can recall. Of smoke and of blood. At night, he shivers, steeped in the terrors of lives so remote from his own, lives he controls with the deft touch of a surgeon

"There can be no forgiveness without forgetting," He says, the mantra meant as much for his apprentice as for himself. The boy watches his mentor scribble a new truth. Choosing what to include, what to change and what to elide entirely. "And that's where we come in."

The boy wonders at his own foggy past, what he has been written to forget. He looks around the ascetic room, a mat, a desk bearing parchment, pen ink and paper, a pool of water at its feet which reflected not the ceiling, but the Historian's world, or star, or void. He struggles to remember, fruitlessly, who he was before this burden was thrust upon him. But there is only emptiness, a hole in his heart hollowed for the pain which will become his burden.

It is the same for all the apprentices. One day they wake in a giant dormitory, sleeping beneath a high glass ceiling, illuminated by permanent starlight. They remember nothing from before, not names, not families. Nothing. They look around, looking at each other in fear, dressed in the robes of the clergy of Historians.

Their stewards, imposing and implacable, tell them only: "This is your life now."

Each is led down a long hallway. Each is assigned a historian, an aged man or woman or other, tasked with watching a small corner of the universe. Many spend every day staring onto planets bereft of life. Either unable to bear it, or it has yet to come, or it has already effaced all trace of itself from history. Each morning they wake; they bathe; they struggle through the fog of children robbed of youth and self, and they are forced to watch the watchers. Some are lucky and see only blackness, or the leftovers of violent death; some are cursed to see civilization in its making or its unmaking.

They learn there is only one universal truth: no more violent thing than life exists. In every form it consumes itself to endure, accruing sin after sin. And that the only way life forgives itself is by forgetting. And that no memory can be unmade.

Therefore... the Historians.

"It is our job to remember," They lecture their young charges. "To witness, and to choose."

"Choose what?"

"Choose what memories the living can bear, and which they cannot. We choose what to erase, to improve. What to take upon ourselves so only our nights are disturbed."

"How long?"

"How long what, my child?"

"How long must we do this?"

Every Historian is asked this question, has asked this question and is ready with the same response.

"Until you are ready to assume our awful responsibility. Until you are ready to keep the universe spinning."

So they watch the watchers, witness their witnessing, absorb their choices, see the universe bend its truth to their pens. And one day, after they internalize the rhythms that keep their corner of existence churning forward without collapse...

...they wake in a Historian's bed.

They look down at their hands, see their decrepitude and wonder if they aged in a night. Or if their mentor's last act was to elide the lives they lived, leaving behind only wisdom.

They look up. A child enters their empty room. Seeing the youths' confusion, empathizing with their fear, they smile:

"It's cleaner this way."

2nd Chance

Simple and useful resurrection app with GPS, Google Maps and e-copy of the Necronomicon

2nd Chance is the first necromancy app available free on your Droid and iPhone (in beta testing stage only)

<< 2nd chance requires a magnetic sensor, location services activated and two samples of blood, one living and one dead >>

This resurrection app is a tool for bringing your loved ones back to life. PLEASE DO NOT USE ON CORPSES DEAD MORE THAN A WEEK. Cannot guarantee that the decedent's soul returns after that date. You may find… another.

1. Although you may bring back to life pets and other animals, they will not know you and must be retrained.
2. Necronomicon is available in Latin only (translations pending)
3. If Location services are turned off, soul may return only halfway. Please keep gun on hand to re-kill any raised abominations.
4. All belief systems supported

The 2nd chance app depends on the performance of your device exactly. If the dead are raised perfectly, it means that your sensors for the nearness of spirits are perfect too.

If there are aberrations, such as the undead (zombies) or manifestations of Beelzebub or Lucifer, please check that you are a firm believer in the afterlife. Any doubt allows for evil to creep through! This app has several options to calibrate your theism (The Bible, Qu'ran and Avesta are all included).

- Pro-version includes:
  - Ø Soul sensor (guarantees accuracy of re-absorption up to 95.5%)
  - Ø Nearest Exorcist locator (in case of resurrections gone awry)
  - Ø Helpful resurrection tips
  - Ø Free vial of holy water

Good luck, and remember, if it's been less than a week. There's still hope. Your loved ones are never fully gone!

John looked down at his phone, then back up at the grave.
Aviva Lester 1988 – 2014
Here lies an angel, returned to God far too soon
R.I.P

Far more than a week, but still, thinking back on the past three years of misery, on the grief that had never lessened, on the unfairness of her dying just after their wedding day, the apps warnings went unheeded as he download 2nd chance and approached his beloved's final (?) resting place.

"I promised," He whispered, "I will never say goodbye."

The app downloaded and stalled, he pulled up its main screen.

SOUL LOCATOR. He pressed the button and, when prompted, enter Aviva's full name and birthdate.

SEARCHING… SEARCHING… SEARCHING…

"Come on!" He begged. "Work goddammit! She's here, she waited for me."

RESULTS: 1 SOUL LOCATED THAT MEETS PARAMETERS. WOULD YOU LIKE TO RETRIEVE? (YES/NO)

John's heart soared. This might actually work. He pressed yes with tears in his eyes.

WARNING. SENSORS SHOW SOUL IS _2_ YEARS PAST 'RAISE BY' DATE. CHANCES OF SUCCESSFUL RESSURECTION <10%. CHANCES OF 'OTHER PRESENCE' USING OPENED CHANNEL ~50%.

DO YOU STILL WISH TO PROCEED? (YES/NO)

"Any chance is a chance worth taking." John said to himself, pressing yes without the slightest hesitation.

The phone whirred for a bit, then grew hot in John's hands. So hot he dropped it into the soft loam of the grave. Blue electricity shot from the phones edges into the ground. Then the heavens opened, and lightning cracked down onto the grave, burrowing into the soil and casting it asunder. The crackling electric bolts struck again and again until a hole several feet deep opened before John, who by that time had thrown himself onto the ground hands before his eyes.

After some moments of chaos, silence reigned. John gingerly took back to his feet, creeping forward to see what remained.

The grave was undug, the coffin struck open, a figure rose unsteadily from it. Rot and years fell away and John recognized his Aviva.

"My God… it's possible. I brought you back. It's possible!" He ran to her, weeping again.

Aviva stared at him silently and with wide eyes, recognition slowly dawning.

"John? But… how. I was, oh my no. I was… dead?"

He hugged her, not feeling the shock of static at her touch. The pain of that was nothing compared to his joy at reuniting with her. "Doesn't matter. Darling, you're here now. I love you. I always loved you."

Aviva's eyes then too began to water. "Oh, John…"

"Come, let's get you home and out of those rags. Everyone will be so glad you're back…"

He half-carried her from the torn grave, as she stumbled over legs rusty from disuse and still-healing rot and atrophy. As he nattered on in his happiness, Aviva turned back the way she had come, eyes narrowing at the sight only she beheld. Briefly, in the moonlight, a translucent figure the mirror image of the girl brought to life reached out towards them. It mouthed silently, no body with which to speak.

John, beloved. That's not me. I didn't make it back. That's not me. That's not me-

The figure faded, its connection to this realm lost. Seeing the figure go, 'Aviva' turned away, satisfied, and once again contemplated what horrors she might work on this world of flesh.

I'm back, baby. I'm back!

The Perfect Fit

There are no perfect fits.

I sit at my desk, haunted by the same page—blank but for a single sentence—on my word processor that's haunted me for months, contemplating my emptiness. I am looking inwards where there used to be words, an endless reservoir I once thought could never run dry, when comes a knock at my door. Opening it, I frown as I see the man with the perfect smile on my front step.

"What do you want?"

"What do you think?"

I cross my arms, defense against the suggestion and the thrill crawling through me.

"I told you not to come here anymore."

His lips curve upward, flashing those perfectly matching rows of pearls, and for a moment I forget how he broke me.

"Let me in." He says, in a voice on the edge of song. One that could always move oceans, especially my own.

Yes. Yes. I almost say, but catch myself. "I can't. I'm writing."

He shakes his head, like a parent who catches their child in an obvious lie. Which—I suppose—he is. "Babe, I'm your editor. If you'd written a word worth a damn in the last year, I'd know."

He steps between the door jamb, and I can smell his breath. Cigarettes and mouth wash and… cheap scotch. Only now I notice how he sways, courtesy of the courage he drank to come here. Sliding one arm around my waist, sending half-forgotten tingles through me, he whispers in my ear.

"Let me in."

"No, I can't. Tonight might be the-" I trail off mid-sentence. What can I say? Tonight might be the night my stories return. Inspiration may yet appear from the emptiness.

Undeterred, he brushes his lips against my ear. He remembers still how to love me; how to play me like he does all others. And how I long to be played, sometimes. I dare not meet his glance, knowing it will captivate me. I dare not close my eyes, knowing that falling into the pool of memory that contains our previous liaisons will do much the same.

"Yes, perhaps tonight the walls fall, and your words return. But that is no certainty. What is certain-" Here he guides my hand to below his belt, and I feel his surging confidence. "-is the void in you *I* can satisfy."

Looking in my eyes, he sees me relent, and he tilts my head upwards until our lips touch. The tingles I felt at his embrace fan into flames. We grow against each other, the bad taste of our history fading away. A distant memory when weighed against the immediacy of our need. He backs me into the bedroom, not letting our mouths part for a second, pushing me there as if by muscle memory. Our clothes drop to the floor, and in a moment, for a brief moment, I am indeed filled. The anguish and the doubt, my failure to create, my anger at this beautiful man chased away by the pleasure and the pain of our coupling.

"You bastard. God damn you, you bastard." I cry. He cannot hear me over the rhythms of his drunken ardor. Whether my tears are born of joy or of sadness, I do not know.

Later that night as he snores loudly beside me, I stare past his slumbering form out the window, up at the blood moon. Pale and red and angry and remote, like our brief passion now when weighed against the cold reality. Any joy I felt at his surprise return to my door fades as the truth returns. Tonight he was mine again, tomorrow he leaves my life and returns… to her. I will be left with nothing but another bittersweet memory. And the void.

"Look at you," I mutter to myself, swimming again in my emptiness, "Gorgeous even in sleep."

I run my hand through his hair, short and dark and soft like down to the touch. He stirs, but does not wake. Closing my eyes, I consider my own ugliness, my fat stunted form cuddled up against his sculpted perfection.

Why are you with me? Someone like me, deformed and unlovable. Why must you torment me with unfulfilled hopes and inspire these unrequited thoughts? I wish… I wish…

Glancing back up at the moon, I finish my thought out loud. "I wish I could know your happiness, and you my sorrow."

Rolling onto my back, the tears return. Silently sobbing, I slip into unconsciousness. A deep, dreamless sleep.

"**WHAT THE FUCK!**" A scream that is at once familiar and yet impossibly strange wakes me with a start. I am in the wrong place. I somehow switched places with him in the night. The scream came from beside me, and so I turn onto my side… and see my own face staring at me in abject terror. I speak again, quietly this time, for it was my own voice that woke me.

"What—what is hap-" Before I can finish my sentence, by some strange instinct, I roll over on top of myself, clasping my hands with a grip that is bigger and stronger than I remember around my own fat throat. I-He look(s) up at me in gasping fear, fat hands trying to peel away my-his own in vain. Before I even realize, I start screaming in his voice.

"You took everything from me! You bastard!" I begin to understand. This is a miracle, my wish. I am become my missing piece. Minutes pass, veins bulging in muscles I am unaccustomed to, eventually he-I stop struggling and go limp, glazed eyes open and staring unfocused at the ceiling.

"You took everything… even the words." I whisper hoarsely, feeling tired and hollow as I stare down at my own corpse.

Disturbed by what I have done, I leap from the bed with a speed and grace I did not previously possess, and stumble down the hall to the bathroom, still undressed. My head pulses and pounds like I am hung-over, but I didn't drink last night. Did I? A memory flashes through my head. I stand at my own door step, hesitating before I knock, spurred onward by drunken desperation.

I have to see him. I remember thinking. *Just one more time. I have to end this life.*

The joy, and trepidation, I feel as the door opens and I see my own haggard, disbelieving face, jolts me back to myself. Opening the bathroom door, I look in the mirror and I see the impossible truth: his chiseled face stares back at me.

Looking at his-my face, I remember more. Drinking at a bar just down the street from my-his apartment, getting progressively drunker as I contemplate how to break free of his-my obsession. I twist the engagement ring on his-my finger as remembrances of our encounters of how my-his words made him-me laugh, twisted his-my heart, completed him-me in a way that no one else ever could. Not even our (our?) fiancée.

And yet he-I must kill me-him. To be free, to return to his-my love unencumbered. So he-I drag(s) our drunken selves up the apartment steps...

Back to the strange face in the mirror, becoming less strange by the minute.

So, the me that is still wholly me thinks, *he intended to kill me?*

We walk back down the hall to the bedroom, seeing what was my body lying there—tongue lolling and lifeless—is a sight I still cannot process. How that heart beats no longer and yet... I am alive?

In a way, I think, with a grin on my-his... on my strange new face, *he succeeded.*

Then I hear it. At first I do not recognize the sound, so long it eluded me, but before long it is unmistakable. I plunge inward, and where for months there had been only silence, a dusty basin devoid of song and of sound, there is a chorus. My words. The light of my life, dark for so long, shining once more. I sit back down at my desk and smile at the sentence, my torment:

There are no perfect fits.

And... and... yes! I can. I can! I begin to write.

There are no perfect fits... and that's okay. We are mere pieces dancing through an emptiness too vast to comprehend, part of a puzzle that is by design incomplete. Our creator, if there is such a thing, is a cruel gameskeeper who has us in a match not meant to be won. But that endless string of loss keeps us searching. That missing fit keeps us hoping that one day—

—our grasp will match our reach.

Then a phone rings. His cell, well... mine now. I step away from the laptop to answer it. I know the name, the man with the perfect smile's fiancée. My fiancée. For a moment it angers the man I used to be, the sad hollow man who chased an impossible dream, one that filled him for only brief moments. Then I realize she took nothing away from me that I did not gladly relinquish out of fear. The love I craved was never truly mine. So I answer the phone, in his strange, sweet, low tone.

"Hey honey." It is, I somehow remember, what he called her.

"Babe? Where are you? You didn't come home after we-we..."

I remember the argument, bits and pieces of my dead lover's life return to me as I need them it seems. They fought before he left her, before he drank up the courage to come and end the part of himself that held him apart from her. Me.

"I… I know. I got drunk and crashed at a friend's. I needed to calm down and clear my head. We weren't very good to each other last night were we?" How easy the words are now; how easy it is to become him.

"No," She laughs, "No I suppose we weren't. Are you coming home?"

"Yes, let me get rid of this hangover, get something to eat, run a few errands. I'll be home this afternoon."

"Okay, I love you."

"I love you too. See you soon." I hang up, and I realize it is true: he loved her. Now I… after a fashion, feel that love too. This woman I have never met, yet I see her perfectly. The separate selves merge together, and only now for the first time do I understand the pain that hid behind my lover's smile. To love this woman and yet… to still need me. A need that ran so deeply he plotted to remove my life from his like a gangrenous limb.

Well, I think, once again looking down at the unseemly flesh that became my bisected lover's grave, *a life has been removed indeed. It would be rude not to claim the opening.*

So resolved, I get ready to leave. I give my old body one last look, not of longing, loathing, not of regret, but of respectful farewell. Despite the hatred I felt for it, it was, after all, the vessel that allowed me to find my passion, where I first heard the words. The words that are as close as I will ever have to a perfect fit. Then I gather my clothes, every hint of my lover—myself that he left at the apartment before I became him. I skip down to the corner-store and buy an accelerant, which I douse everything with, leaving a trail out to the kitchen.

I light that with a match, and make my quick escape from the building.

Driving his… my car away from the sirens, the smoke, towards *my* new life. I contemplate the pasts. I have two of them now, one that belonged to the man I was, and one that belonged to the man I am becoming. I can remember more and more of him, as if the world senses that this is who I must be.

I look to the future, to the fiancée I return to, to the child I now remember grows inside her, my child. Closing my eyes, I can picture holding her in my arms. Somehow I know it will be a daughter. I can see her grow, and the joy we take in her maturing. I see myself filling my love in moments of passion, the way I was once filled by the body I inhabit. I see myself still sneaking off to be filled by other men in the venal, necessary way that part of me that is me still craves. I see us happy, despite the shadows that haunt every marriage. I see her catching me in quiet moments, when I look up at the stars and become a man she doesn't recognize, or I say things entirely out of character for the husband she thinks she knows. I see her asking me what's wrong, time and time again, dissatisfied by my bizarre non-answer. It is the only one I have.

We are old in one of these visions. Our daughter long gone with a wife and kids of her own. I sit by the lake behind the home we bought to grow old—and die in—together. Sitting on the pier, I do not hear her approach, but she can see the look on my face, another one of those that is not her husband's.

She sits beside me, resignedly, and sighs, saying only: "You know, when we were young, I was so sure you would tell me what was wrong. It must have happened that day."

I turn to her in shock: "What day?"

"There was a day, a day you change, before we married. We had a fight and you left for a night. You said you went to a friend's, but…"

"But?"

"You came back, and I was glad you came back. But after that day you were different somehow. Not worse, better in fact, just different. It was after then you took up writing for yourself. Who knew you could be so good at it?"

She pauses for a moment, resting her head on my shoulder. I start to run my hands through her hair, even in brilliant white it is still beautiful.

"Still, I thought… though it doesn't really matter, does it? I thought you would tell me."

I take her chin in my hand, and turn her towards me. We kiss, one of tens of thousands to happen between now and the end. Alas, all I have for her are the same words. There are no more to spare.

"My dear, you already know what I'm going to say."

"Say it anyway, the mystery is a comfort now. Something I know will never change."

I sigh, I always sigh, though now, with her understanding, it hides a smile.

"In the best stories, the main character always has a secret. One that only he, or she—"

And here, I sneak a secret look up at the sky. Up at you.

"—and the reader know."

Made in the USA
Lexington, KY
07 February 2018